Trouble At Timber Ridge

KEVIN CRISP

Trouble at Timber Ridge

Western Trail Blazer
ISBN-13: 978-1494742218
ISBN-10: 1494742217

Copyright © 2013 Kevin Crisp
All rights reserved
Cover Design Copyright © 2013 Karen Michelle Nutt
Design Consultation by Laura Shinn

Licensing Notes
All rights reserved under U.S. and International copyright law. This book may not be copied, scanned, digitally reproduced, or printed for re-sale, may not be uploaded on shareware or free sites, or used in any manner except the quoting of brief excerpts for the purpose of reviews, promotions, or articles without the express written permission of the author and/or publisher.

Trouble at Timber Ridge is a work of historical fiction. Many of the important historical events, figures, and locations are as accurately portrayed as possible. In keeping with a work of fiction, various events and occurrences were invented in the mind and imagination of the author and are interwoven with the historical facts.

Trouble at Timber Ridge

Harlan Shea receives a message asking for help from an old friend. In spite of secrets from the past he'd sooner forget, the big man rides back to Timber Ridge.

Possible rustlers, an unusual telegraph clerk, and a few old enemies lead to several questions and more than one shooting before Harlan begins to figure out what is happening.

Then the trouble gets downright serious when Shea meets a beautiful woman with secrets of her own.

*For my dear wife Tracey,
whose encouragement, patience, and support
made writing this book possible.*

*A special 'thank you' to Jack Legg
for sharing his knowledge and editing skills.*

Chapter 1

Coming dusk began to cloak the lonely trail through the pine woods of the front range mountain foothills in sinister shadows. A single rider, whose breadth of shoulders made him appear oversized even for his great horse, was in no hurry to breach the wood line into the plains beyond. No stranger to the darkness, the giant with black Stetson tipped forward low over his brow held the reins laxly with his left hand. He seemed to guide his horse along the long-unused trail by force of will. His posture was slightly hunched, the habitual pose of a tall man accustomed to ceilings and doorways not made to accommodate height like his. A bystander might have mistakenly thought the man was dozing, so at ease was he. But not a sight, sound or scent escaped the stranger's wolf-like senses.

Moments later, his gun barked. A timber rattler that had issued a warning a few yards in front of the horse jumped and then fell, writhing in death throes. A peregrine falcon lifted off its perch on the man's shoulder and rose, riding the wind's currents, then darted forward. Long, powerful talons snatched up the still writhing snake, and the raptor vanished into the leaves above.

"Enjoy the grub, Horace," murmured the rider, continuing down the trail.

The trail soon opened into cleared foothills where scattered cattle grazed. The yellowing grass, cropped low by the herd, was balding in places where hooves had pounded the growth into submission. Not far from the woods, a few cowpunchers retired their horses and dusted themselves off as they awaited the dinner bell at the bunkhouse. A few dogs milled about, tails wagging and tongues lolling in anticipation of the table scraps to come.

The cowboys stopped when one of them noticed the big man riding toward them and called to his companions. Instinctively, fingers reached for their pistols. The dogs growled, unsure what to make of this shadowy form. To both man and animal, the rider presented no immediate threat, but something about him suggested an underlying menace.

"Howdy, stranger," the foreman said, stepping forward cautiously. A falcon, part of a dead rattler dangling from its talons, swept over the cowpokes' ducking heads and perched on the ranch house roof. "What the devil was that?"

"Peregrine falcon," the rider said.

"Does it belong to you?"

"No, I wouldn't say that."

"Name's Johnson, I'm foreman 'round here. What business brings you to Timber Ridge?"

"I'm Harlan Shea," the rider said. Dismounting, he handed the reins to one of the ranch hands. The horse shifted her weight and stomped her hooves. "Think your boss is expecting me."

There was an immediate change in the tension in the yard. The ranch boys let their hands ease off from their pistol butts. Johnson nodded. "Go right on to the house there. We've been expecting you for ... for some time now."

"Corral my horse, would ya, but be careful. Delilah here ain't completely broke." As the man turned and walked toward the door of the ranch house, the dark mustang stomped and snorted indignantly.

Shea banged a big fist on the heavy door of the ranch house. A servant led Shea to a fire-lit room, fragrant with the sweet smell of burning pine. The ranch owner, Glen Haxton, sat at the head of a long, wood table, beginning to take his supper.

"Well, if it ain't Harlan Shea," Haxton said around a generous bite of stewed beef, which he promptly washed down with a slug of redeye. "Lord, have you grown since I

Trouble at Timber Ridge

last laid eyes on you? Harlan Shea, come to solve my problems."

"I got your letter," Shea said, retrieving a folded paper from under his knee-length leather coat.

Haxton grunted. "Which one? I've been sending letters all over Colorado for weeks, hoping one of them would fall into your hands eventually. Sit and have some grub."

"I haven't been in towns much."

"Where have you been?"

"In the mountains, mainly. But I trek in for supplies once in a while. The general store manager in Chester knows me and held your letter for me. Wouldn't have gotten it otherwise. I wasn't expecting no letters."

Over six and a half feet and nearing 260 pounds of lean muscle, Shea seemed to dwarf the dining room, even while he sat. The cook flitted about between the men, stepping over dogs while dumping heaps of steaming stew into shallow tin bowls. Biscuits were heaped around the heavy table. "A lot of new faces in your yard, boss," Shea said. "Can't say I recognized any of them."

"The old crew moved on not long after you left," Haxton said. "The new foreman couldn't control them quite like you, so I let them go. They were wild – untamable. That old life is behind me now, and that's just as well. My riding days are done." He lifted a cane that leaned against his chair to emphasize his point.

"It still worries you, does it?"

"The hip? Damn. It'll never heal. I'm a crippled hound, though my bite still hurts, don't it, Bennett?"

"It shore do, boss," the cook answered on his way out of the room.

"You seen any of the old boys since?" Shea asked.

Haxton tore off a chunk of biscuit with his teeth, chewed it for a few moments, then shoveled it into his cheek with his tongue. "Ricky and his brother swung by the neck for horse thievin'. O'Brien was stabbed in his bed by a whore in Colorado Springs the fall after you left. Dan stuck around for a couple of years. He saved my life, you'll remember. On account of him I'm limping rather than staring up at the roots of grass." He washed the biscuit down with more liquor and slammed the finished glass on the table. "He met a girl and I gave them a little parcel of land and some cows for a wedding present. He's just over yonder," he gestured noncommittally with his fork. "The rest of them was bad, Harlan, but you know that. I imagine the balance of them is in hell or well on their way."

Shea finished mopping up the last of his stew with a chunk of biscuit and graciously accepted a second bowl from Bennett, who was making his way back around the table.

"These here boys are different, though, Harlan," Haxton continued. "Ain't a bad apple among them. They drink a fair bit and raise hell in town on occasion, but it's all good boyish fun. I'm through with outlawry, and if any of the ol' boys save for Dan and yourself set foot on my property again they'll eat lead. Unless, of course, they could convince Johnson out there they was lookin' for an honest job in less time than it took me to draw."

"Did Johnson overlap with any of that crew?" Shea asked.

"Not all that long," Haxton answered. "Johnson is still pretty green. But he does your job okay."

An awkward silence followed.

"So, you gonna tell me why you sent for me?" Shea asked.

"That's how I remember you, Harlan. Right to the point." Haxton refilled his glass of liquor and slammed down another gulp. "I'm damn near broke. Haven't sold any cattle for months. But that's not what the buyers say. According to them, they've received a shipment from me by rail as recently as a few weeks back. I think someone is selling cattle in my name.

"I remember how you handled those Heinz twins back when they was rustlin' me and you were foreman here. These new boys, Harlan, they're hardly the type to take on outlaws. Time was when a cowboy on this range took the law into his own hands. Now, we got Sheriff Reddington in town; law and order reign, and we're powerless to defend our interests.

Trouble at Timber Ridge

"Business is changing 'round here too. I can't make heads nor tails of any of it. When I was a young pup, long drives and Indian fighting made a man a man. When you did business, you did it face to face. Put your cards all down on the table where the other guy could see them. But today, the cattle business is all telegrams and rail cars."

"I thought I saw telegraph poles in the distance as I rode up."

"Did you come up through town?"

"No, I came the other way, from the mountains."

"Hmm..." Haxton paused a moment to wipe his mouth with his napkin. "Damned eyesores. Wasn't so many years ago this was all free range, remember? Why, you were here when the Y Bar O started building its first fence.

"Well, as far as Johnson can tell, not a cow's been stolen from my herds. But a couple months back, the buyers stopped replying to my telegrams. I haven't made any deliveries, and money's getting tight. Those boys out there are getting antsy; they haven't been paid for long enough, I reckon a few are thinking of leaving. I've got one or two empty bunks down there as it is.

"I sent Johnson to see Fairbault and find out why the buyers stopped contacting me. Johnson told me his conversation with Fairbault was downright strange. Fairbault seemed to have no idea anything was irregular. And he gave Johnson this." Haxton pulled a telegram out of his vest and slid it down the table to Shea.

> PAYMENT FOR ALL SHIPMENTS DIRECT TO
> TIMBER RIDGE BANK STOP FB HAXTON
> FULL STOP

"I take it you never sent this telegram," Shea said.

"No, I didn't."

"So somebody's forging telegrams. And unless you're considerably changed from the man I knew, you still keep your funds in mattresses, hollowed out trees and under floor boards – never in bank accounts."

"Damned if you could even guess how many stashes I've got! Some old habits die hard," Haxton grunted.

"Fairbault showed Johnson a lot full of my brand, but Johnson said the brands looked sorta blurry."

"Blotted?"

"Maybe. Johnson wasn't sure. Like I said, he's young and got no experience with rustlers. But his counts add up, and he's checked and re-checked them. As far as he can tell, we're not missing a steer.

"Shea, you don't owe me anything. And I'm still not sure if I did the right thing kicking you out. But if you help me, I give you my word I'll make it worth your while. You know I pay fair."

"Guess I can stay on here for a spell," Shea said, mulling the mystery over in his mind. "Sure sounds curious. Forged telegrams, blotted cows. Somebody out there's pretending he's Glen Haxton. I suppose a crooked feller could make a few bucks selling cows in your name for a while, but why? Why not just sell straight to the buyers? I never heard of anybody blotting brands to make them look like someone else's cows. More regular just to add 'em to their own herd."

"It's awful peculiar, ain't it?"

"Could do some heavy damage to your reputation if your buyers began to suspect you of cattle rustling."

"Johnson said Fairbault never brought that up particularly, but the man was a heap cautious and reserved. You think someone's trying to ruin me?"

"You've made enemies in your time, boss."

"That I have."

"One in particular comes to mind."

"He's crossed my mind too. Reckon that's the main reason I called you. If it's him, I'll need all the help I can get."

"Well, I don't suppose I've anywhere else to be for a while."

"So, you'll take the job?"

"For the time being."

"When can you start?"

"Night's still young. Think I might take a stroll through town." He made his way around the massive pine table for the door.

Trouble at Timber Ridge

"That's the Shea I remember! So, you'll start immediately. But wait, Shea, hold on."

The big man paused with his hand on the door.

"You were a damn fine foreman. Was the liquor what made you do what you did, I know that. And, well, it's fine to see you around my table again."

"Okay," Shea said, and pushed his way through the door and into the crisp evening air.

Chapter 2

Johnson stood alone in the yard, arms propped up on the corral fence, watching the setting sun and chewing the last hunk of biscuit from his supper. "Will you be needing your horse, Shea? Or shall I show you where to bunk?"

"My horse, thanks. I know the way to my bunk."

Johnson deftly leapt the gate, cautiously approached the mustang, and gathered the reins. He unlatched the gate from the inside with his free hand. Shea saddled Delilah, and gave the straps short tugs to make sure all were snug.

After a moment, Johnson asked, "Shea, do you think the boss is right that Gust Lundgren may have something to do with all this?"

"How much do you know, Johnson?"

"I know the boss can't sell his cattle. I know Fairbault suspects maybe he's been selling some rustled cattle. And I know somebody's been sending telegrams in the boss' name."

"So, you know 'bout as much as me."

"I guess so, then. Mind if I ask what he was like – the boss? You know, years ago."

"He was a fighter. Terrible to his enemies. Feared and respected. But around the campfires at night, he often talked of a quiet life on a peaceful ranch somewhere."

"And Lundgren?"

Shea grunted. "Terrible too – a mean man, right down to his very bones. Never did see eye to eye with Haxton. He talked of ranches too, someday, but as sort of a legitimate cover to his outlawry."

"Were you here during the shootout with Lundgren?"

Trouble at Timber Ridge

"That happened the summer just before he let me go. Hotter than hell, that August."

"Must have been something awful."

"We were holed up in the old bunkhouse for about three days, taking shots at them through chinks in the timber. Two men died the first day, and by the third day they started to bloat and smell. Nothing to eat, and but half a bottle of liquor to quench six men's thirst. We slept in shifts, relieved ourselves through holes in the floor.

"The third night, one of Lundgren's boys — new fella, one we didn't recognize — threw a lit kerosene lamp on the roof from behind, set the whole place ablaze. This forced our hand and we tore out into the yard, guns blazing. They rushed us at the same time. That's when Haxton took a bullet through his hip at close range. Would have killed him if Dan hadn't thrown himself on Lundgren's arm. Risked his own life to save the boss."

Both men's eyes drifted to a rectangular, bare patch of stony ground. Charred stumps of foundation timber surrounded the scar in the yard, beside which lay several graves, with small cross markers.

"Did Dan Waldschmidt run with Haxton's gang?"

"Dan and his brother were orphaned. They were taken in by various folk over the years. Ranchers, shopkeeps, whoever had heart or need of them. They were split up most of the time. Eventually, Cody Waldschmidt, the younger brother, found a more or less permanent home at the Y Bar O. But Dan kept raisin' hell, and kept getting kicked out of places. Eventually, Haxton took him in and whipped him into shape.

"Haxton could tell there was some good in him. Looked to us like a fellah who wanted to be an honest man. He was in need of a good job, so I hired him."

"Boss never talks about the fallout with Lundgren," Johnson said, hoping to prompt an explanation.

"No, that doesn't surprise me," Shea said, half a smile on his face. "Lundgren could never prove who'd robbed him, but he was sure Haxton was behind it."

"Boss sure was anxious for you to come back," Johnson said awkwardly.

Shea put his hand on the man's shoulder. "Listen, you oughta know I've got no mind to take back the job as foreman."

Johnson showed his relief.

The falcon swooped down from his perch on the ranch house roof. Johnson ducked and swore as the low diving bird's tail feathers knocked off his hat and the bird of prey landed on Shea's extended forearm.

"Doggone beggar, you are," Shea said, pulling a small scrap of jerked beef from his pocket. "Snake meat wasn't enough to fill your belly, eh?"

"That's some bird," Johnson said, noting the falcon's evil little eyes scrutinizing him over a small, gnarled beak.

"This here's Horace. I figure he's half falcon, half demon. He ain't my pet. We just happen to share a trail." As though on cue, Horace flew off into the dusk.

As Shea headed down the well-trod trail toward town, Johnson called after, "Why don't you stick around for a bit? The boys are up to a game of Liar's dice just now. Someone'll spot you if you're empty. We'd love to hear tell of the boss in the old days."

"Another time, perhaps. Tonight, I'd like to have a look around town. It's sure been a while." Shea glanced over his shoulder, and thought Johnson had something more he wanted to say, but nothing was forthcoming.

The trail to town hadn't changed since Shea left town years earlier. "Feels like old times, eh, Delilah?" he asked his horse. The rising moon cast long shadows that deceived the eye, making the patches of scrub brush alongside the hoof-cleared path seem to grow as he watched. The path was steep and rocky in places, coming to its low point just across the creek from the town. It was an easy crossing, except just after the snowmelt when the creek swelled to flood levels. Scattered pines and rocky rises studded the foothills, which changed to snow-capped mountains a short ride away.

The little town of Timber Ridge had changed though, tethered now as it was to the lifelines of modern technology. The long line of telegraph poles running up and down the railroad track looked to Shea like giant

Trouble at Timber Ridge

fencing corralling the town. The sleepy village showed evidence of nocturnal life. Kerosene lamps burned brightly outside thriving businesses. Candles glittered in the hotel and boarding houses. Shea noted the depot was still open at the other end of town.

Shea tied Delilah outside O'Malley's saloon. He checked his pistols before mounting the steps. The big man drew considerable attention as he entered the saloon. A hushed silence came over the drinkers and gamblers when Shea pushed through the batwing doors. Cards froze in mid-play, poured drinks missed the glasses, and cigarettes burned forgotten in tobacco-stained fingers, as folk sized up the huge stranger striding to the bar.

After a moment, relief and recognition flashed across O'Malley's face. "Well, if it isn't Harlan Shea. Big as a bull, and I almost didn't recognize you! Don't just stand there, old boy, have a seat. What can I set you up with?"

"Got any coffee?"

"It's cold, leftover from breakfast, and burnt to hell. But sure, if that's what you're wanting, it's on me." Signs of normal life returned to the saloon with the reassuring signs of familiarity between stranger and barkeep. Slowly, others began to recognize Shea, whom they'd not seen for years. Some, like a couple of riders from the Y Bar O ranch, looked none too pleased at Shea's unexpected return.

O'Malley poured the grainy dregs into a tin cup for Shea. "Where have you been these long five years?"

"Around. I take it no one's come by asking about me of late?"

"I imagined you didn't have much trouble landing a position on another outfit somewhere."

"I've been here and there."

"Sounds interesting." O'Malley paused a moment waiting for more. When no elaboration was forthcoming, he asked, "What brings you back to Timber Ridge?"

"I'm presently in Haxton's employ."

"Finally saw the error of his ways, huh? If you ask me, he was a damned fool to let you go in the first place. You were falsely accused, and everybody 'round here knew it."

"I never denied anything."

"Well, one way or the other, I'm sure glad to see you back. Excuse me a moment. The new girl's late again, so I'm workin' the tables." O'Malley hurried around the corner of the bar and off through the tables, collecting empties and taking orders.

Shea slurped down the thick, tar-like coffee. "Strongest stuff I've drunk in years," he muttered to himself.

O'Malley was back in a minute. "So, how's Johnson taking to being replaced?"

"I'm not replacing him."

"Good for Johnson since he can barely pay his debts with his current pay. For a while there, he'd be in here every night at cards. Altogether, I understand he owed the Y Bar O outfit upwards of six months wages. That boy doesn't know when to quit, either at cards or at drink, a greenhorn through and through. Don't tell me Haxton has you working under him!"

"I'm not working the line at all. Just looking into some of Haxton's affairs, at his request."

"Yeah, I've wondered if everything was all right on that side of town. The boys don't come down here that often anymore. Hard to say if something's up, since Haxton holds his cards close to his chest. His whole operation is run on whispers and nods, more like a gang of outlaws than a ranch. But I've had the sense something is out of place."

"Know anything about it?"

"No, but I reckon I might know someone what does." O'Malley lowered his voice. "There's a stranger who's been coming to town frequently as of late. Tall man, and thin. Dresses like a gunslinger and keeps his mouth shut. He sits over there in the corner. He can keep sitting there as long as he keeps drinking, but I don't like the looks of him. He was here one evening when Haxton came in for a nightcap, and boy if he didn't slither out the door slick as

Trouble at Timber Ridge

a sidewinder. If you stick around a bit, he usually comes in just after dark."

Shea slugged down the rest of the coffee, "I'll keep that in mind. Thanks for the coffee. I've got some business down at the depot I oughta look into before the agent closes up for the night."

"Well, take 'er easy. And Harlan – welcome back."

"Thanks." Harlan headed out.

Chapter 3

The depot was a long wooden building with peeling gray paint beside the railroad track. Heavy cans were stacked along the wall, alongside bales of unprocessed leather. The empty passenger's waiting room was lined with benches, along which folks tended to huddle around a big, black pot-bellied coal stove in the winter.

At the north end of the building was the depot office. Through the barred ticket-agent window, Shea heard the clacking of a telegraph. A posted placard listed rates for express freight service, passenger service, post, and the Western Union. A train order hoop leaned up against a corner beside the office door.

As he approached the windows, Shea heard hushed voices within. "I won't, Alvis," a woman's voice said.

"I can support us," a man's voice replied. "Industry's booming; jobs are opening up everywhere."

"But anywhere you can get a job, he could find us," the woman continued. "It's no use running. Besides, don't you know your reputation will follow you? All we can do is see this through..."

The whisperers simultaneously noticed the dark shape eclipsing the ticket window. The telegrapher was a pale, red-haired fellow, his freckled face colored with the urgency of his conversation. Sitting on a small, gray-blanketed cot tucked into a tight corner was a young, slender brunette with striking blue eyes. She was very beautiful, and her straight posture and calm demeanor suggested an inner strength of will.

"How long have you been standing there?" the telegrapher asked, embarrassed. "I hope I haven't kept you waiting long."

"Long enough," Shea said.

Trouble at Timber Ridge

"I was just leaving," the young woman pardoned herself. She stood, straightened her ankle-length skirts, and began to collect her things.

"Are there any outstanding telegrams for delivery to Mr. Haxton?"

"No, but even if they were, they'd need to be delivered into his own hand."

"I see. Well, while I'm here, I'd like to send a telegram," Shea said. "To Arnie Fairbault."

"The cattle buyer? Okay, sure. Let me grab my ledger." The telegraph agent stepped to the desk in the corner and grabbed a leather-bound logbook from where it lay amidst keys and clicking sounder boxes. In the cramped little office, the telegrapher and the girl stepped around each other in an awkward dance as she made for the door and he for the barred service window.

"What would you like the message to say, stranger?" the young man asked, recovering his professionalism.

"My boss would like to sell 400 head in a single rail shipment, available to ship immediately."

"And your boss is?"

"Mr. Haxton, of course."

It seemed to Shea for just an instant that both the girl and the telegrapher hesitated. Then, the telegraph agent penned his entry into the logbook. "All right then, '400 head available immediately from Haxton to Fairbault', will that be all?"

"Did I say 400?" Shea asked, "I meant 500." Annoyed, the telegrapher busied himself with correcting his ledger. The door beside him opened, and the girl brushed within inches of Shea's sleeve. "Don't believe I caught yer name, Miss."

Shea's steel gray eyes were fixed on the soft, fair face of the girl. Her cheeks pinked. She smiled slightly as she replied, "I don't believe I gave it." Then, she stepped past him and out of his view. But the outline of her figure left an impression in Shea's mind's eye that burned long and stubbornly, like an ember in a dying campfire.

Turning back to the window, Shea found the telegrapher's face veiled with jealous anger. "And who shall I note is sending the message?" he asked. His voice was tense, though he struggled to control it.

"Mr. Haxton."

"I'm sorry, sir, but I cannot record the name of the sender as anyone other than the sender himself. That would be fraud, sir."

"And of course that never happens," Shea finished the sentence for him.

"I'd lose my job, sir—" He stopped suddenly.

It seemed to Shea that, from behind him, the girl communicated with the young man in one of those subtle ways women get a word into a conversation before they open their mouths.

"If you'll just give me your name, sir, I can send along this telegram first thing in the morning."

"I'm Harlan Shea." This name provoked no reaction from the telegrapher, but behind him, the rhythmic stepping of the small, light feet approaching the door seemed to hesitate, and Shea took note. The door opened behind him – *rather quickly*, he thought – and the girl stepped out into the night.

Shea took a handful of coins out of his coat pocket, carefully counted out the fee, and slid it under the bars.

"Nice doing business with you, Mister...?" Shea said.

"O'Connor," the telegrapher replied. "Alvis O'Connor."

"All right, O'Connor, I'll be back to collect the reply."

Outside the depot, there was no sign of the girl. "The young lady left in quite a hurry," Shea muttered. He glanced over his shoulder toward the depot, and thought he could make out the telegraph agent staring into the darkness through the window.

"Those two are up to something," Shea said. Habitually, his hands checked his pistols.

-*- -*- -*-

On the other side of town, the girl hurried up the steps of O'Malley's, pausing a moment to catch her breath, adjust her hair and straighten her skirts. Deftly, she tugged at her clothes until she looked presentable. She swung open the batwings and stepped inside.

Trouble at Timber Ridge

"You're late," O'Malley said, hustling between tables and wiping sweaty palms on a dirty smock tied around his waist. "These tables don't work themselves."

"Sorry, Mr. O'Malley," she said. "It won't happen again."

"That's what you said the last time," he muttered.

She grabbed an apron off the bar, threw it over her skirt, grabbed a bottle of liquor, and strode immediately over to a corner table, where a tall, dark man leaned his chair back against the wall. His hat was tipped low over his face. His well-worn black boots crossed on the table. Heavy pistols hung low from his hips, dangling over each side of the chair. Wisps of blue smoke drifted around the rim from a red-tipped cigarette dangling from his lip. His arms were crossed. An empty tumbler sat on the table in front of him.

"Another drink, sir?" she asked.

The man grunted, and she poured. Her hand shook noticeably, and a trickle of redeye poured down the side of the glass. "There we are," she said, as she placed the half-empty bottle on the table beside the glass. Then, in a low whisper, she added, "We may have trouble, Oswald."

Chapter 4

Louisa was right. Harlan Shea was a problem, and not one Oswald was prepared for. He'd heard his employer utter Shea's name with strong emotion on many occasions, and the boss was not one to cower in the face of an adversary. Oswald watched the girl flutter from table to table, masking her discomfiture with short-lived smiles and small talk with customers. Even as he hungrily devoured her lithe young form with his eyes, his mind mulled this new information and what it could mean for him.

Oswald knew Shea had roots in these parts, but Oswald understood that when he departed he'd left with dishonor and bad blood. Why return after all these years? Perhaps, he came back to seek revenge on Glen Haxton, who ruined Shea's local prospects with a rash and very public firing. That was an appealing thought, as Oswald knew precisely which end of the barrel he wished to be standing on when Shea drew his guns. The idea that Shea and he might be fighting on the same side was appealing, but somehow he didn't think that very likely. The dust of Shea's falling out with Haxton had likely settled by now. If Shea waited this long to get revenge, he would have waited for a reason.

Could be he was planning something big, Oswald thought. *Was Shea planning something ruinous, even fatal for Haxton?* A small, humorless smile crossed Oswald's face. He had no particular grudge against Haxton. For Oswald, Haxton's undoing would be merely a means to an end. He'd only seen the man a few times. On the first occasion, Oswald made a half-hearted attempt to burn Haxton alive. No, Oswald had nothing personal against

Trouble at Timber Ridge

Haxton, but Oswald rarely had anything personal against anyone he robbed or murdered.

On the other hand, Shea could be just passing through Timber Ridge on his way somewhere more fruitful. Timber Ridge was a growing town, but held little promise for a shamefully fired ex-foreman. Also, the timing was suspicious. Of all the small towns in Colorado, there was almost no chance Shea would cross this one now, when Oswald was there working.

No, Oswald was certain that if Shea was back in town, old wounds must have healed, and Shea must be connected to Haxton's interests. Almost certainly, this put Shea at odds with him, and these were not odds in Oswald's favor. Oswald sucked absently at his cigarette until the burning embers singed his fingers. "Damn," he said.

The stakes were too high at this point in the game for Oswald to tolerate another player. Shea needed to be eliminated, but Oswald doubted he stood much of a chance of besting Shea in a fair fight. Of course, he wasn't above bushwhacking an adversary. And that was what he figured to do. Oswald would love to be able to brag he beat Shea one on one, but considering Shea's ability with pistols, that was decidedly lacking in appeal.

Oswald would keep an eye on Shea, figure out where he stayed, which trails he rode, and when he was likely to be alone. Then he would set an ambush. He wouldn't rush it, though. He wanted to learn what Shea was doing back it town. Shea – and Haxton, for that matter – might suspect what Oswald was up to.

Oswald raised his empty tumbler to summon Louisa. As she started to pour his drink, he lit another cigarette, speaking out the side of his mouth as he did, the way men learn to communicate in the penitentiary. "Keep him busy for now," he told the girl. "Don't care how you do it or what you have to do. I need time. You just keep him distracted until I get rid of him." With that, he got up and left her standing there, still holding his filled glass.

-*- -*- -*-

In the morning, Shea woke up confused. He rubbed his eyes, wondering if the last five years had been a dream, if he had never fallen out with Haxton, if he'd been at his ranch all along. Here he was, in his old bunk again at the Haxton ranch. He could hear the cattle mooing mournfully on the hills and smell the manure and the neighboring pines. Then, there was a fluttering of wings as Horace flew up and landed on the windowsill above his bed. "Morning', Horace. Looks as though you've had your chow." As though he understood, Horace slurped up the bit of field mouse tail dangling from his hooked beak.

Shea stumbled to the washbasin and splashed a bit of tepid water on his face with cupped hands, drying his face on his shirt. Glancing around, he saw that all the bunks were empty – the entire outfit must have poured out without waking him. "Boy, I'm out of practice," he muttered. "Or, at least it's been a long time since I slept in a bed with both eyes closed." He strapped on his holsters with twin Smith & Wesson Sheffield's. Over these, he threw on his long, leather duster.

Across the valley, the long string of telegraph poles stretched from hill to hill, and Shea wondered what messages could be heard in those lines this morning. He recalled the telegraph agent's whispered conversation with the beautiful, mysterious brunette with the blue eyes. There could be an awful number of things a fellow would want that young lady to do which she might find disagreeable. He wondered what she'd objected to last night when Shea interrupted their little tête-à-tête. The memory of the girl thrilled him. Although he only glimpsed her for a moment, those high cheekbones beneath sky blue eyes and the thick, wavy dark hair cascading over her creamy white neck haunted him. He felt an irresistible desire to see her again, and wondered briefly if today's tasks would bring him near to her.

From his chair on the ranch house porch, Haxton hobbled up beside him on a crutch, smoking his morning pipe. "Morning, Shea. Gettin' lazy in your old age, are ya?"

Trouble at Timber Ridge

"Better night's sleep than I'm used to, I guess."

"Late night at O'Malley's?"

"I stopped by there briefly, caught up with O'Malley. You know, barkeeps are all ears and wagging tongues. But he didn't seem to know much. Bank was closed, so I stopped by the depot to meet the telegraph man."

"Arrogant little weasel, isn't he? Seeing him parade around town with Louisa is enough to turn any man's stomach."

"Is that the name of the beauty with the brown hair and the blue eyes?"

"Louisa Campbell. Quite a looker, isn't she? Serves tables at O'Malley's. I don't think even a whore would be better for business than having her pour the drinks. She came through not long after the telegraph agent arrived. Half the outfit has called on her, but it seems she only has eyes for scrawny, red-headed sophisticates."

"He doesn't seem likely to make friends around here."

"Well, he doesn't belong here, that's for sure. Seeing those two sitting in the gazebo on Sunday afternoons, him reading her poetry from some old, stuffy book and her all kinds of sweet on him, it's an insult to manhood. These young city chaps, they're just not made of the same stuff as the rest of us."

"I sent a telegram to Fairbault claiming you had 500 head ready for the rail line."

"Okay, I reckon I could hold to that. Do you think he'll remember you?"

"Fairbault? Not sure, we met once. But I would like to find out if he gets the message. Or at least, how it reads when he gets it."

"I see what you're getting at. Damn, why didn't I think of that? You're suspicious of the telegraph agent already, ain't you?"

"Well, I've got my eyes open, and everyone's fair game right now," Shea said, mounting his horse.

"I took him for a little pain in the butt, but never thought he would have the balls to do me wrong."

"You're probably right. My gut tells me that if he's in on whatever is going on around here, someone bigger is calling the shots."

"Let me know what turns up."

"'Course," he said, patting Delilah on the flank. "Come on, Horace." The large falcon flew to Shea's extended forearm.

"Now, how'd you train that bird to do that?" Haxton asked, amazement obvious in his voice.

"Train nothing. Horace here does as he will." Shea started down the trail, but after a few paces, he called back over his shoulder, "But I suppose it helps that I keep little scraps of jerked beef in my pockets." He could hear the rancher's deep, belly laugh as he trotted away. Horace rode along on his shoulder until he got to the creek, and then he flew off after some small, pitiful bird in the trees, which probably never saw him coming.

Chapter 5

The bank was a modest affair, laid out like a general store but for the large safe behind the desk. Nailed up along the walls were yellow, brittle wanted posters. Shea inspected them discretely but thoroughly. Some had faces he recognized, but his was not among them. A couple were men he had killed.

The banker was a slight, bald little man of indeterminate age, whose crouched posture over the desk suggested a miserly disposition. He did not even look up when Shea's heavy boots clunked across the creaking floorboards.

"Good day. You open? I'm here to make a deposit," Shea said, dropping a small sack of coins on the banker's counter with a resounding thud.

"Do you have an account with us, Mister...?" The banker waited expectantly, but without looking up from the notes he was making in his ledger.

"Name's Shea. Harlan Shea. No, I don't have an account, but I'd like to deposit these funds into Mr. Haxton's account."

"I'm sorry, sir, but Mr. Haxton does not have an account with us." He pushed the money sack back across the counter.

"I see. So, if I wanted to deliver a small payment to Mr. Haxton, what would you recommend?"

The banker replied, "I suppose you'd have to ride up to his ranch and see him, as he doesn't like to bank here. It isn't far. Just west of town, up the hill."

"Guess that's what I'll have to do, then. Thanks." Shea turned and started for the door.

"You know," the banker said, "as far as I know, you're the first who's ever even asked to deposit money for Glen

Haxton. If I didn't know better, I'd suspect he'd turned legitimate."

"He's changed, but it still doesn't surprise me, I guess," Shea said. "He's old-fashioned. Doesn't trust other people to manage his money."

"I was surprised and pleased to see that his new foreman has a more modern perspective on banking."

"Mr. Johnson keeps an account here?"

"He does."

"Does he check his balance often enough to notice if I made a deposit?"

The banker looked up at Shea, eyeing him suspiciously. "He's in regularly enough. He's due to come in to withdraw the outfit's pay tomorrow. Whether Haxton likes it or not, he tells me."

"Well, perhaps I'll leave the coin in Johnson's safekeeping then."

The banker opened the pouch, and counted quickly. "Shall I make out a receipt?"

"Please."

The banker scribbled onto a small page, signed and folded it, and gave it to Shea. "Your money is secure with us, Mr. Shea. We have quite a nice vault back there, the finest they sell. Mr. Haxton apparently doesn't concern himself with minor matters like protecting his funds, which would be much safer in there than under his pillow, or wherever he keeps it. The outfit's lucky to have Johnson. They can thank him for ensuring they get paid regularly."

"Yes, they can thank him for that," Shea said, tucking the receipt into his vest pocket.

"Good day, Mr. Shea."

"And to you," Shea said. Then, much quieter, he muttered, "You've been very helpful." Shea wondered if payment from Fairbault was being deferred to Johnson's account. Was Johnson pocketing the outfit's pay? Was he the one who sent the fraudulent telegram to Fairbault?

Something didn't quite fit, Shea decided. If Johnson forged the telegram, why did he willingly hand it over to Haxton? And how was there money in the account for

Trouble at Timber Ridge

Johnson to withdraw? Haxton said he'd not sold any cattle for months.

Outside, the sun was warming the chill morning air. The shrill sound of a train whistle cut through the quiet, followed by the thundering chug of powerful pistons. Shea stretched and walked to the train station, glanced at the incoming freight train, and stepped into the depot. O'Connor was in an obvious panic behind the window, reading ticker tape and scratching notes hurriedly on paper. Clanging sounders and clacking keys created a cacophony.

"Good morning, O'Connor," Shea called.

"I'll be a few minutes. Hope you can wait."

"Something wrong?"

"Northbound is early and the station boss is late. Sleeping it off again, I imagine. Now I've got two trains headed opposite directions on the single rail. Gotta send this one into the siding or there'll be an awful wreck." He pushed quickly through the office door, leaving it slightly ajar, and darted for the trackside door.

Shea waited a moment, and stepped into the depot office. O'Connor's ledger lay open on the desk. He quickly glanced down at the most recent entries. He found the message he paid for the previous night. But it was not the original, since there was no crossed-out '400' on the page.

"A couple reasons a fellah might keep two sets of books," Shea said to himself. Could be the telegrapher was meticulous, and worried about records being lost or damaged. O'Connor struck Shea as quite meticulous. But it could also be that there was some value to him in keeping two versions of the same records, and this possibility piqued Shea's interest. Quietly, he slipped out of the office, closing the door behind him.

The Baldwin 2-6-0 locomotive billowed gray smoke as it slowly coughed through the crossing, the whistle screeching and the bell clanging. The sand and steam domes, bell, and smoke stack atop the boiler reminded Shea of uneven teeth, jutting out at eye level with the tall cab like some hideous under-bite.

He chuckled as he watched O'Connor struggle to hand off the paper train order with a long-handled loop. O'Connor had to run about half the length of the depot alongside the locomotive before the fireman managed to grab hold of the order through the window. At this point, O'Connor tripped and fell on his face. The train began to pick up speed again, and the black smoke belched into the air. The cattle in the freight cars mooed in discontent as the train passed out of site around a hill.

"Here, let me lend you a hand," Shea said, walking over to O'Connor, who was kneeling in the dirt, still clutching the loop. Shea pulled the young man to his feet, and swatted carelessly at the dust on his vest. "Some job, eh?"

"Some days, anyway," O'Connor said.

"I was just stopping by to see if Mr. Haxton's telegram to Mr. Fairbault had gone out okay."

"Sure it did," O'Connor answered, with what Shea thought was a touch of resentment in his voice. "I sent it up this morning first thing, just like I said I would."

"And how do I know if it was received?"

"Mr. Shea, telegraphy is my expertise. You'll just have to trust that I know it as well as you know ... whatever it is you do."

"You'll have to excuse me, O'Connor. I'm just used to dealing with people I can look in the eyes."

"Yes, that's a nice way to conduct business. But my way is faster, and the modern world doesn't wait for handshakes and pleasantries."

"I suppose that's true. I'll check back again tomorrow to see if a reply's been received. Will you be around all day?"

"I take my lunch at noon."

"Good to know," Shea said, strolling away. He stopped at the bank, untied Delilah and walked her down the road to the hitching post in front of O'Malley's Saloon. The smell of bacon filled the air with a rich, savory aroma, tinted with the scent of maple.

O'Malley's was empty, save for the new sheriff, a rotund man named Reddington, who nodded at Shea as

Trouble at Timber Ridge

he entered as though to say, 'I recognize you're here, but I'm eating.' Shea nodded back, and took a seat at a different table.

Louisa, she of the shining dark hair and big blue eyes, was refilling Reddington's coffee cup. She turned and gave a little start as she recognized Shea. It was only a moment, though, before she regained her composure. She walked with an exaggerated wiggle to her hips as she strode to his table.

"Well, hello again," Shea said.

"Mr. Shea, is it?"

"Please, call me Harlan."

"All right, Harlan. What'll we be having this morning?"

"That bacon smells right good, and a few cups of coffee to wash it down."

"I'll be right back," she said, tossed her hair with a touch too much flamboyance and strutted back to the kitchen. Her slim waist and generous hips kept Shea's attention. A moment later, she was back with a hearty serving of heavily-salted, thick-cut bacon, biscuits, and a steaming cup of coffee with bits of crushed eggshell still in it.

"So, you're O'Connor's girl, is that it?"

She started a little once again, and Shea couldn't tell if she was acting or not. "Well, I suppose I am."

"You two engaged or something?" Shea said, taking a rather large bite of bacon.

"Excuse me, but that's getting rather personal."

"It's just that you strike me as a kinda bred-in-the-west type of girl, and he seems more..." Shea struggled for lack of words.

"Sophisticated?" she supplied. "Cultivated?"

"I was thinking snot-nosed easterner, but 'sophisticated' will do for now."

She looked a trifle indignant. "There's a lot to Alvis most people don't recognize. You'd be surprised what he's capable of."

"Would I now?"

"He comes from a good family in New York, very high society."

"I thought he was from St. Louis."

"Well, he was born in New York, but his father raised him in St. Louis. His father is the president of a trade union."

"Couldn't be that high society then, if he works for his meat."

"Well," she said, becoming flustered, "higher society than is to be found around these parts, anyway."

"And you're the type of young lady who's impressed by that sort of thing."

"Alvis is unlike anyone I've ever known. And he's smart, very smart."

"That's good. When trouble comes to town, he can find a clever place to hide."

She laughed. "Mr. Shea, I'm beginning to think you're having fun at my expense."

He smiled gently. "Sorry, miss, I'm just unaccustomed to conversation with a girl. Seems I've been up in the high country on my own too long."

"I'd suggest you're a hermit from a previous era, if you didn't look to be just a little older than I," she said. "Women invest their hearts somewhat differently than you men think, Mr. Shea. Our mothers may have wanted the tough, strong pioneers. But those days are gone and the brilliant men of industry are our suitors of choice these days."

Shea chewed his bacon thoughtfully, and washed it down with a gulp of coffee. "I knew a smart fellah once. Too smart for his own good, I'd reckon. Had wits and strength and shot a bullet straight and true. Quite the hellion, he was. Name was Gust Lundgren."

Her expression betrayed her surprise.

"Oh, he was a pile smart," Shea continued. "Robbed banks, rustled cattle, kidnapped ranchers' daughters, held up stages and trains. Never was caught neither. Raised hell all over Colorado. You can see his picture hanging up still, on the wall at the bank. Just saw it there this morning, with a generous reward posted beneath it. See, miss, in my opinion, if a man has no soul, neither brains nor brawn will save him."

Trouble at Timber Ridge

Louisa quickly checked her reaction. "Mr. Shea, I have to get back to work. Perhaps we can continue this conversation some other time."

"Do they still have that visiting parlor over at the hotel?"

"Yes, they do."

"And is that where you're staying?"

"It is."

"Well, how 'bout I drop by this evening and pay my respects. Nothin' improper, just a friendly visit."

"That will be fine," she answered.

Too quickly, Shea thought. "And Alvis won't mind, will he?" He watched her eyes carefully. He thought there was a touch of hesitation in her response.

"Of course not. It's quite a respectable hotel, and the parlor's perfectly public."

Shea stood, and dug in his pocket for the coins to pay for his fare. She was tall, he noticed, as most women he had known were like mere children beside him. His broad chest and huge arms could fairly crush her slender form. But she did not seem intimidated by his imposing stature. Rather, she stood in front of him, looking up into his face with a gaze full of curiosity, but devoid of fear. She looked as though she might say something more, then abandoned it, took the change from the table, and returned to the bar.

He lifted his hat and called after her, "Good day then, Miss Louisa."

"Good day, Mr. Shea," she called over her shoulder without looking back.

Outside the saloon, the street was filling with the bustle of weekday business. Mr. Haig swept the stoop outside the general store. Sheriff Reddington, having breakfasted quite well, had taken up his vigil outside, leaned against the saloon's facade, looking bored and important. Haxton was pulling up to O'Malley's in the buckboard.

"Mornin', Harlan."

"Mornin'." Shea gave the crippled man an arm getting down from the buckboard. Haxton took the assistance with dignified reluctance.

"Found something out this morning, boss," Shea said, in a low voice. "Seems our telegraph man keeps two sets of books."

"How'd you find that out?"

"When I telegrammed Fairbault yesterday, I changed my original message before I left. He had to cross it out and rewrite it, but the book out on his desk today didn't have any corrections."

"Just played a hunch, did ya?"

"I don't trust men who do business without looking a fellah in the eye. A couple years ago, there was this banker up in Lonsdale who kept two sets of books. He shuffled numbers around to cover up the fact he was borrowing funds to pay off some bad debt."

Haxton smiled. "Was this fellah a business partner of yours, Harlan?"

"Let's just say he was an acquaintance."

"Someday I hope you'll fill me in on what you've been up to these past five years."

"Someday I might."

"Well, what do you think these two sets of books mean?"

"Not sure, yet. May have nothing to do with your problem, but it sure gives me cause to keep an eye on O'Connor."

"Sounds like. Anything else?"

Shea hesitated. He did not want to incriminate Johnson until he knew the full story about the bank account and those biweekly withdrawals. "I gotta hunch maybe Louisa back there has got some connection with all this. Might go over and visit with her this evening so we can have a proper chat."

Haxton's face darkened. "You watch out for that one, Harlan. Girl like her can make a man forget his loyalties." The rancher turned and limped his way into the bar.

Chapter 6

A few yards away, Oswald concealed himself behind a stack of crates in the alley by the side of the saloon. He smiled to himself. This was precisely the type of opportunity he was looking for. If Shea paid an evening visit to Louisa, it might be a valuable chance to take a shot at him from concealment and, more importantly, a good chance of getting away under cover of darkness. All he needed to do was pick one of the many convenient spots where he could watch the hotel entrance and wait for Shea to end his visit with Louisa. He could as easily shoot Shea on the way into the hotel, but Louisa might learn something from the meeting that may be of use.

Not that he was happy about the idea of Shea playing the gentleman caller to Louisa. Perhaps it sickened him even more than the thought of her tossing about in the hay with that little red-headed man-child, Alvis O'Connor. Her infatuation with O'Connor would abate, he figured, once she saw him for the weakling everyone else knew him to be. Although Oswald could rarely comprehend what women saw in men, he was keen enough to realize Shea's strong jaw, gray eyes, and broad shoulders had the potential to weaken a girl's will.

Furthermore, Louisa was every bit the type of woman who evaded Oswald. No stranger to the ladies, most of his familiarity with the gentler sex had been through establishments where the evening ended in payment rather than passionate embraces. Louisa's straight posture, upturned chin, and fighting will invigorated a man, even a bad man, to attempt the impossible. And Oswald knew from reputation that Shea was a man well acquainted with the impossible.

As soon as Shea was out of sight, Oswald crept out of his hiding spot and headed for the wood line behind the town, where he met Johnson. "You kept me waiting."

"I've more important business to attend to in this town than you," Oswald said mockingly.

"This is the last payment I'll be bringing you until you make good on your word," he said, scowling.

"Easy, Johnson. I'm working on it, but that's quite a sum you've got need of."

"I mean it. This is the last withdrawal until you pay. If you don't pay by next week, I'll empty the account and use that to pay off my debt to the cowhands at the Y Bar O."

Oswald grimaced. Truth was he had no intention of paying off the Y Bar O boys on Johnson's behalf. He hoped to drag his feet as long as possible. Eventually, the whole game would start to come apart, and when Oswald hit the trail, he wanted the payment promised to Johnson to still be in his pocket – a little bonus his employer need not ever know about.

"Johnson, you're not in any position to threaten. If word gets out you're withdrawing pay for the outfit and pocketing it, what exactly do you think Haxton's boys will do to you? Be honest – you're lucky that loose-lipped banker hasn't let anything slip yet."

"I'm not stupid, Oswald. I know you won't blow your cover until every penny's been transferred out of that account to your boss. This is it. Last payment. Make good, or the account's shut up tighter than the knees of a..."

Oswald struck Johnson hard across the jaw, knocking the foreman over. The cowboy was right. He needed Johnson, and hated him for it.

Johnson was no stranger to fist fights; his head came back up quickly and he recovered his balance. Johnson slammed a fist into Oswald's gut that winded him and brought his head down. Stepping back, the cowpuncher hit Oswald across the jaw with a solid right.

Oswald stumbled, half stunned.

Trouble at Timber Ridge

Johnson was a natural fighter, but he was also a proud man. Even without an audience, Johnson was not one to fight dirty. Fists up, he gave his opponent a moment to recover.

But Oswald was not above fighting dirty. As soon as his vision stabilized, he lunged at Johnson, taking him down with a shoulder to his stomach as he tackled him. Pinning Johnson, Oswald brought his knee down hard in Johnson's gut, and pounded the foreman a few times just below the eye and on the side of his throat. Satisfied with the pain he inflicted, Oswald stood and kicked Johnson twice in the ribs as he lay groaning. At least he could remind the insolent cowpuncher who was in charge.

Johnson rolled over onto his belly and coughed. He managed to tuck his knees under him as he gripped his aching abdomen. To Oswald, he looked like a toddler sleeping with his butt up in the air. "That should teach you not to step outta line," he said, leaving the moaning man sucking on dust.

This whole business stunk, Oswald reflected, as he walked out between the buildings and headed toward the depot. There just was not enough money changing hands to make the game interesting. He'd made his boss more than twice as much with just one holdup as he had to gain here. Hell, this was less than he'd tried to steal from the boss five years earlier! But for this heist, he needed to depend on a cocky cowpuncher and a nitwit telegrapher to hold together an elaborate scheme that permitted just a small, discrete trickle of funds to his employer. Minus his cut, of course, which was not much. Worse than that, pretty little Louisa, who had been immune to Oswald's advances since she was old enough to flirt, seemed to be falling for tenderfoot O'Connor. And, Harlan Shea, notorious gunman, had come into town looking for trouble, with a confrontation seeming inevitable. How was any of this worth the effort, or the risks?

When he met the boss, Oswald had been nothing more than a small-time cattle rustler. Oswald quickly learned the boss had loads of cash buried, and set out to discover where by secrecy and deception. His loyalty to his boss was opportunistic – he sought to protect his employment just long enough to rob his employer. In the meantime, the boss had seen Oswald's potential, and together they did great things.

But the current job wasn't even a decent-paying train robbery – not even a holdup – it was a small-time job. It infuriated him, even as Oswald was smart enough to know revenge rarely made for profitable business. Besides, there were quite a few players this venture depended on – like the one bleeding in the dust behind him. The more players, the more hands could be misplayed, but Oswald was hardly in a position to raise objections. After all, the falling out that precipitated this plan was mainly his fault. The best he could do was play along and pretend he knew nothing of the truth.

A train disgorged a small number of passengers and their parcels onto the platform as Oswald arrived. A few folks were meeting family members, and a couple of business-looking types headed right for the hotel. One caught Oswald's eye. He was an older, bespectacled gentleman with scraggly white whiskers and a shiny bald head. His eyes were keen and observant. There was no sign of a weapon beneath his coat, but that didn't mean he didn't have one. Many such men carried pocket pistols or derringers. Curiously, a pair of field glasses dangled about his neck. He strode directly to the station boss.

"I say, are you the stationmaster here?" There was an eastern lilt to his speech.

"Close enough," the boy answered.

"I'll need a horse and directions to the Haxton Ranch."

"Is Mr. Haxton expecting you? Perhaps he's sent someone to pick..."

"No, he isn't, but I should like to make my presence known as soon as possible."

There was no doubt in Oswald's mind. This man was a cattle detective. Clearly, he was not the run-down-the-rustlers-single-handed type of cattle detective Oswald had been expecting, but he had an air of authority about him. Oswald stepped discretely off the platform and disappeared into the crowd. As he did, a smile cracked

Trouble at Timber Ridge

his chapped, tobacco-stained lips. Perhaps the boss' plan was going to work after all. And the sooner Oswald could finish this job and get back to snooping around for the boss' hidden riches, the better.

Chapter 7

Shea lunched early, and took Delilah out for a long ride around the pastures. Periodically, he examined the brands on Haxton's cattle, but they were all clean with sharp edges seared neatly into cowhide. For hours he searched and counted, but never once did he find a blemished brand. Then he rode back to the ranch house and checked his counts against Johnson's. "He's telling the truth, anyway," Shea muttered to himself. "Haxton's not been rustled. Something else is going on."

Shea found the bunkhouse empty when he returned. He shaved off a wealth of scraggly stubble that seemed to have been there since the last time he glanced in a watch glass, whenever that may have been. He washed his hands and face, and picked the dirt from under his nails with the point of a hunting knife. It was getting on late afternoon when Johnson entered, watched him silently for a moment, and then asked, "Big night?"

"I'll be payin' a lady a visit," Shea replied.

"My word, man, you've only been back in town a day. Boss never mentioned you were such a ladies' man."

"This lady might know a pile more about the cattle operations than befits a saloon girl."

Johnson thought for a second. "Wait, who's the gal?"

"Louisa Campbell."

"Ah, Louisa. Well, I sure as hell wouldn't mind spending an evening discussing ranching with her, or just about any other topic."

"What happened to your eye? Looks like you've been kicked by a mule."

"Just clumsy, had a bit of a fall," Johnson uttered quickly. "What of Louisa's redheaded beau? Won't he mind you calling on her?"

Trouble at Timber Ridge

"Not sure whether he knows," Shea said. Then he added suggestively, "Some people keep secrets, even from the ones they're closest to."

Johnson reddened. Unconscious of his response, his eyes roved over to his bunk, where his bedroll and meager possessions were laid out.

"Anything you want to tell me, Johnson?"
"About what?"
"Well, money for starts."

Johnson's upper lip quivered as he said, "Speak clearly, Shea, I don't know what you're getting at."

Shea pulled a folded receipt out of his pocket, and handed it to Johnson. "I left you a little something this morning." Shea kept one eye on Johnson's hand, but it showed no creep toward his holster, nor did his thumb show the telltale twitch.

Johnson sat heavily on his bunk, head in his hands and receipt still between his fingers. "I don't take you for a thief, Johnson," Shea said. "But I got a hunch you know more than you've been letting on."

"You're wrong, Shea. I don't know nothing more than what I told you about the boss' cattle, sales, or anything else. This is an embarrassing personal matter."

"Gambling debt?"
"How'd you know?"
"I asked a lot of questions in town."

"It's that loose-lipped O'Malley," Johnson said, a touch of indignation in his voice. "I know it. He'd betray Peter to Paul."

"So, you owe money, is that it?"
"To the boys over at Y Bar O."
"And you can't pay it back out of your own funds?"
"Not a chance. Not if I saved up for years."
"Whose money is that down there in the bank?"
"No idea."

Shea stared at him. "How'd you come by it?"

"I didn't. It was deposited shortly after I opened the account. I told the banker I'd be using the account to pay wages to the outfit. I was told not to ask any questions about where it came from."

"You're using it to pay back the Y Bar O, but you don't know whose it is? And taking out payday-sized amounts so the banker doesn't suspect anything?"

"You're right about part of it, but I ain't paying down the debt. I'm handing the money over to some middle man who's passing it on to somebody else."

"You're funneling money to somebody who doesn't want the world to know they're getting it. Any idea who?"

"No. Honestly, Shea, I've got no idea. The middleman's name is Oswald..."

"Oswald again," Shea interrupted.

"You've heard of him?"

"A few times now."

"Anyway, Oswald said he'd pay off my debt to Y Bar O. All I have to do is withdraw amounts from the bank and hand them over to him, until the account dries up. The payments would be decent size, roughly what a banker might expect to be withdrawn to pay the ranch hands, so as not to draw suspicion. Then, he'd give me a lump sum to get me out of trouble with Brelje's Y Bar O outfit."

"Any idea who he works for?"

"Nope."

"I'm guessing he's the fellah what busted your eye?"

"We had some disagreement about the timing of my payment. You think Oswald's connected with this cattle problem the boss has?"

"Call it a hunch."

"Then, I reckon I'm in a heap of trouble."

"That's a feeling I'm familiar with." Shea put a hand on the foreman's shoulder. "We all make mistakes. Life has a way of giving men a second chance, if they're smart enough to change their ways and take it. Just look at the boss, or myself, for that matter. I bet you'll land on your feet."

"Hope you're right."

Shea headed out into the yard. Johnson followed a few paces behind. "Shea?"

"What is it, Johnson?"

"Is it true? About you robbing Lundgren? About you being the reason Lundgren and his gang rode up from

Trouble at Timber Ridge

Texas to kill the boss? Did the boss fire you after the shootout with Lundgren because he knew you were the cause of it?"

Shea was silent for a long while. Finally, he said, "I've never denied it."

"Gives me hope, you coming back here after all these years and starting over. I think I could use a new start too."

"Good luck, Johnson."

"Goodbye, Shea."

Horace swept down from the roof onto his extended arm. "You old bastard, you're gonna ruffle me up. Don't you know I'm off to see a lady?" The falcon screeched defiantly, and clung to his perch awkwardly as Shea mounted Delilah and trotted down the steep path to town.

Chapter 8

Haxton sat at the table in the ranch house with the detective, Sydney Perloe, whom Fairbault had called in on behalf of the Cattlemen's Association. The conversation was uncomfortable, and punctuated with a good deal of reviewing documents and scribbling notes on Perloe's part. As the detective studied his documents, Haxton watched the perched spectacles slide steadily down the long, beak-like nose until they threatened to plummet off. Then, with clock-like precision, Perloe would nudge them back into position with an ink-smudged finger. Moments later, they would commence their descent once more.

"You sure you're a cattle detective?" Haxton asked, studying his visitor.

"Whatever do you mean?" Perloe asked over the rim of his spectacles, but without any real defensiveness in his voice.

"Well, you just don't look the Pinkerton type."

"Oh no, I'm quite another breed of detective altogether, if I do say so myself." He removed his spectacles. "I like to think of myself as a connoisseur of intrigue. I have traveled extensively around Europe and India, in pursuit of embezzlers and larcenists of all types. And I pride myself on my many successes, all owing to my peculiarly inquisitive mind and refined sense of deduction."

"And what brings you to the American west?"

"Well, a man of my respect and reputation," his emphatic gesture bumped his coffee and would have spilled it, had it not been for the quick reflexes of the rancher, "is offered many choices of places around the world in which to practice my art. But I have passed by

Trouble at Timber Ridge

many an opportunity to practice in some more exotic urban locale owing to my other great passion."

"Which is?"

"Ornithology."

"I don't know what that means."

"Birds, my good man! The diversity of avian fauna. From the gold-crested black finch to the tree-climbing kestrel to the ground-nesting hawk, is there any finer place about the Western Hemisphere to watch birds than the great American West?"

"I guess I hadn't noticed," Haxton replied.

"Why, just on my quick jaunt over here from the station, I was blessed to see several lark buntings, and I do believe I heard in the distance the distinctive vocalization of a canyon wren."

Haxton harrumphed. "I ought to introduce you to my former foreman. Why, he's trained a falcon to perch upon his arm."

"A falconer? In Colorado? My word! When I was last in England, I accompanied a gentleman in pursuit of that magnificent diversion, along with a contingent of traveling Mohammedans. Fascinating sport, quite invigorating. What's your man's name?

"Harlan Shea."

Perloe paled. "Not the Harlan Shea!"

"You know of him?"

"He's notorious in other parts. Has word of his exploits the last few years not yet reached the sleepy town of Timber Ridge?"

"Perhaps not."

"Well, it's too long a tale for the moment. But I implore you, Mr. Haxton, if you have any passion for justice, to please keep him on hand at least until I've had the opportunity to pass along word of his whereabouts to my associates over in Lonsdale."

"Is the law after him? What has he done?"

"Let's just say that the law is interested in speaking to him. And, I might add, your association with him does not necessarily help your case to clear your name in the present matter. In light of the fact, I would urge future

- 45 -

cooperation in this matter of the Shea investigation, following up promptly with any and all requests for information concerning him which may be forthcoming."

"I'm not in the business of turning loyal friends over to the law, Perloe."

"Nor are you in a position at the present time to be uncooperative. Now, back to the business at hand, Mr. Haxton. Your buyers are truly quite concerned about this recent sale of apparently brand-blotted cattle, which you claim neither to have shipped nor to have been paid for."

"It's understandable that this would all raise a few eyebrows. I hope your investigation will prove I am the victim of this crime, not the perpetrator."

"Time will tell. Truth can never be hidden for very long. If you are guilty of a rustling operation, I must commend you on the cleverness of the cover-up. It may prove among the more original and bold plots I've had the pleasure to unveil." Perloe jotted down a few more notes. "Well, at your earliest convenience, I'd naturally like to tour your herd and inspect their brands."

"Of course."

"Naturally, I don't expect to find anything untoward."

"You don't?"

"If you are guilty of rustling, I hardly expect you'd keep the stolen cattle amidst your regular stock," he said, repositioning his spectacles. He paused a moment. "Unless, of course, you were clever enough to hide stolen cows in plain sight." Perloe studied Haxton, as though he expected to discover something in Haxton's expression, but Haxton's face revealed nothing other than perplexity.

"Well, we shall see then," Perloe continued, peering over the rims of his slipping glasses.

"My foreman Johnson can take you out to see the herd. There's plenty of time yet before dinner."

"Ah, yes, that will be very good. Shall we?"

The two men strode together to the bunkhouse, with Haxton slightly in the lead. Haxton knocked as he simultaneously pushed the door, and called, "Johnson, you in here?"

"Is he not in?" Perloe asked.

Trouble at Timber Ridge

Haxton's eyes landed on Johnson's empty bunk. His bedroll and meager possessions were gone, and there was no sign the bunk had been recently occupied. "He's gone," Haxton said, half to himself.

"Jumped ship, did he?" Perloe said. "Curious timing, indeed."

-*- -*- -*-

Alvis O'Connor jumped when he looked up and saw Oswald standing at the window. "Good Lord, Oswald. Why must you always creep up on me like that?'

"Got a minute?"

"Sure, come on in," O'Connor said, opening the door to the small telegraph office. Oswald strode in, sat in O'Connor's chair, and clunked his heavy boots up on the desk.

"Shea been by here yet?"

"The big fella? Yeah, he's been snooping around a bit, asking a pile of questions. Who is he anyway?"

"He's kinda the reason we're here."

"How so?"

"Shea's the fella Haxton ordered to rob Lundgren a few years back."

"That so?"

"That's why Lundgren went after him with the outfit a few years ago. Lundgren and Haxton, they was business partners of a sort. After some years and considerable profit, Haxton wanted to retire. He spent much of his share of the loot buying the ranch just west of Timber Ridge and a herd, but then he got greedy.

"Lundgren had a heap of gold back in those days, stashed in a few spots Haxton found out about. Haxton sent Shea after one of particular significance, and stole a heap from Lundgren. So, Lundgren and the rest of the gang went after Haxton. The resulting shootout lasted some days, and Lundgren almost finished Haxton, but for Dan Waldschmidt interfering. Lundgren only managed to cripple Haxton, rather than kill him.

"Haxton's a sly one, you ought to know, and he quick made like he had no idea Lundgren had been robbed. He's never admitted anything, made like Shea was operating renegade. Fired him, and nobody's seen Shea for years, 'til now."

"How much gold did he make off with?"

"More than we'll ever get from the current job." Oswald's voice dripped bitterness.

"Was this gold from a job Lundgren and Haxton worked together?"

"No, it was mainly from jobs we pulled down in Texas."

Parts of these revelations tantalized O'Connor. "Did you know where your boss hid his gold?" he asked.

Oswald laughed. "You're awful smart, Alvis." Oswald fingered the butt of his pistol. "If you're as smart as I think you are, you'll shut your trap before you start making costly implications."

O'Connor swallowed. "Why do you suppose he's come back? Think he's trying to make good with Haxton?"

"Not sure," Oswald said, rising to his feet. "Whatever the reason, I'll rest easier once he's out of the way."

O'Connor looked up at him, uncertainly. "But how...?"

The tall, dark gunslinger made no reply.

O'Connor added another point to his long, mental list of reasons not to cross Oswald.

After a pregnant pause, Oswald said, "It's come to my attention that you've been thinking about skipping town."

O'Connor turned scarlet. "What? Where did you get that idea?"

"Don't play the fool with me, O'Connor. I know you're considering eloping with Louisa."

"You've been listening in, haven't you?"

"I've been looking out for my employer's interests."

"Is that all?"

"My employer wants me to inform you that he feels your relationship with his daughter is growing a bit too serious for his tastes."

O'Connor's eyes burned with hate. "Oh, your employer wants you to inform me, is it? I'm not blind, Oswald! I've seen how you leer after her."

"A beautiful woman is like a fine horse, O'Connor. You can strut around with her proud as a cock, but a fine

Trouble at Timber Ridge

horse draws thieves like a carcass draws buzzards. You can't keep an eye on her all the time. How long do you figure you can keep her under lock and key, boy? If I was you, I wouldn't get too comfortable."

"You're wrong, Oswald. She's sweet on me, and she'll marry me yet."

"If she cares for you at all, she'll save your neck by refusing your proposal. You've been warned." Oswald rose and left the office. "And I wouldn't leave town, if I were you – not before this thing's seen through," he added over his shoulder as he stopped a moment at the door. Then he walked out the door and into the dusk.

Chapter 9

"Miss," Shea said, removing his hat as he ducked into the low ceilinged parlor of the hotel.

Louisa rose. "Mr. Shea. It's a pleasure to see you again."

"Yes, well, you'll have to excuse my manners, Miss," he said, turning his hat in his hands. "There ain't been many gals for me to talk to these last few years, and I've grown a bit coarse."

She smiled. "I understand from Mr. O'Malley that you haven't been back to Timber Ridge in a long time. In a sense, I guess that makes us both newcomers."

"I guess."

"Please, have a seat. By the fire, where it's warm."

He sat silent and imposing on a chair across from her. Another guest shuffled into the room with a newspaper under his arm and a pipe in his hand. He awkwardly surveyed the strained, intimate scene for a moment, and then left as discretely as he could.

"Have you been traveling these past years, Mr. Shea?"

"No, ma'am, not really, although I've been about, here and there. As long as I've lived, I've never been out of sight of them peaks yonder," he gestured vaguely toward the mountains.

"A child of the west you must be," she said.

"Yes, I suppose you could say so."

"What brought you back to Timber Ridge after so much time?"

"I came back to help a friend."

They were quiet for an uncomfortably long minute. Then, she asked, "Mr. Shea, I was surprised when you asked to call on me tonight. Pleased, but surprised. You'll

Trouble at Timber Ridge

forgive me if I say so, but you don't seem the gentleman caller type."

"What type would you call me then?"

She looked him up and down. Hard-muscled and sturdy, he looked every bit as unconquerable as the mountains. She mused that he could snap her like a twig, if he felt so inclined. She smiled, figuring she could have him in her thrall before long.

Then as quickly, the smile faded. Louisa reflected how a wild beast might feed from your hand one moment then turn savagely upon you the next. She examined his heavy pistols as they lay in their holsters. "You look the gunfighter to me, Mr. Shea. A loner, perhaps a drinker, and a gambler. A man whose womanly companions are usually ... less than respectable."

"Well, I haven't had strong drink in a few years, and I've never been one to go in for whoring, but I do come from a long line of fighters. My granddad was a fearful Indian fighter, back in those days, and every bit as terrible as the savages he fought. My father told me that during one particular raid, a tomahawk glanced off granddad's temple, knocking him unconscious, but failed to wound him mortally. When he came to, an Indian witch, naked as a newborn babe, was chanting over him. He couldn't understand her, but somehow he knew she was laying a mighty curse over him and his line. We've been restless wanderers, plagued by conflict, ever since."

She laughed sweetly. "I've heard similar yarns from the mouths of other men. Those stories are fairly common down where I grew up. I don't believe in curses, Mr. Shea, except maybe the kind men bring upon themselves."

She thought he looked a little hurt at this. "I'm sorry, Mr. Shea. I shouldn't go casting aspersions at your family legends. I suppose every line has pride in its tall tales."

"I'd wager your family may have similar stories."

"Why would you say that?"

"Call it a hunch."

She paused reflectively for a few moments. "Why did you come to see me tonight, Mr. Shea?"

"Please, call me Harlan."

"Thank you. You may call me Louisa. Why did you come calling on me tonight?"

"From the moment I saw you, I knew I had to speak with you alone," he said.

"My, you are coarse," she said. "And forward."

"My apologies, once again, Louisa. Like I said, I've been in the wild country a long time. I've seen some troubling times these last few years. I've forgotten the niceties of civilized living. I've become accustomed to fighting for what I want and need."

"Is the law after you?"

"In some parts, I suppose they are. But I can't take credit for all they've laid against me."

"Perhaps you are cursed after all, Harlan Shea."

He turned his Stetson in his hands. "Perhaps we have that in common."

"Whatever do you mean?"

"Louisa, you are probably the most beautiful girl I've ever had the misfortune to lay eyes on. It's a singular beauty you have, something truly rare. Why, that dark hair and pale blue eyes, I can't remember ever seeing the like, but in one other."

Louisa smiled, as much with her eyes as with her lips. "My word, an old lover out of the life of the infamous Harlan Shea. Do tell me all about her."

"Weren't no her at all, Miss. He was an outlaw, black of soul, a killer through and through. Wore his dark brown hair a touch on the long side, with piercing blue eyes that could look right through you."

Louisa shifted in her seat uncomfortably.

"Reckon you could pass for his daughter. His name was Lundgren. Gust Lundgren."

The room became awkwardly silent, with only the crackle of pine and birch in the fireplace offering any contribution to the conversation.

Finally, Shea said, "Your name ain't Campbell, is it Louisa?"

"Have you come to pay your respects, Harlan, or have you come to question me?"

"Maybe a little of both."

Trouble at Timber Ridge

"Well, enough about me, at any rate," she said. "Let's talk about Harlan Shea. Why, yours is practically a household name."

"That so?"

"I know a pile more about you than you do about me, I'll wager. I know you've done a fair share of killing and stealing in your day. I know there's at least one price on your head."

"I wonder how you know that."

"Why, everyone knows about it, don't they? How you rode down to Texas and hid in the scrub brush for days, watching and waiting for an opportunity to do your master's bidding. How you waited until Lundgren and his boys went away on business, and then you dug up his wife's grave..." She began to choke up slightly, fires of rage burning deep in her eyes. "Dug up the coffin in the middle of the night, while her daughter slept soundly just across the yard. It was heavy, I'm guessing, heavy for the coffin of a woman who died of consumption. Heavy with gold from a jackass mail wagon the boys robbed outside of San Antonio.

"You're loyal, Harlan, I'll give you that. Would have turned the stomach of any sane man, violating a grave like that. I figure you'd have done just about anything for Haxton, and the unappreciative old man fired you anyway, just to take the heat off him."

"Louisa, there ain't nothing I've ever done in my life that's been any other's bidding than my own. I may have worked as Haxton's foreman, but I've only ever been my own man."

She reddened, beautiful in her fury as she struggled to get her emotions under control. "I wonder how you knew to dig up her grave."

"I wonder what kind of man buries his treasure with his dead wife."

She bit her lip to cool down. Then she straightened her skirts and her silky hair, and with remarkable coolness, continued, "So, Haxton ordered you to rob the grave, left you high and dry afterward, and made like the whole operation was your idea."

"As I said, Haxton never ordered the job."

"I have a hunch he did. Somebody must have found out something. Pa wouldn't have let on to the locations of any of his stashes, not unless drink got the better of him. Who were you working with, Harlan?"

"Would it matter?"

"It might," she said meaningfully. "And I have another hunch."

"What's that?"

"I have a hunch you're still a pile angry at Haxton for putting the blame on you. Your job, your friends, your community, your home, your name – he cost you all those things didn't he?"

"Yes."

"That's quite a price Haxton exacted from you. He betrayed you, his loyal foreman, for how many years? How many times did you risk your life for Haxton, only to be betrayed when trouble came? I bet you'd love a chance to get even."

"Would I?"

"A man deprived of his work has cause to be enraged. But he did worse than that. He ruined your reputation for miles around. No one in Colorado would hire you once they heard about the hell you brought on Timber Ridge, would they? So, you wandered the wilderness, hungry and poor for years, until like a lame dog you came crawling back begging to your master for a handout. I'm betting, Harlan, that if an opportunity came along to put things right, you would take it."

"What are you getting at?"

"I have a friend in town who could help you. He has an interest in setting things straight."

"His name Oswald?"

She smiled, rose from her seat, and took her place beside him on the couch. "Just look at you, Harlan Shea. What are you doing working for that crooked old rancher anyhow? You're feared throughout these parts today, but that will fade the longer you play the part of manservant to that old cripple. You're back here for some reason, aren't you? Maybe not a conscious reason, but something

Trouble at Timber Ridge

drew you here after all these years. Some unsettled business, some score to settle, perhaps?"

"Maybe I came back to put things right with Haxton."

"I don't think so. You don't seem the remorseful type."

"Maybe he hired me to finish off Lundgren."

She tensed, then caught herself. "You're a killer, Harlan. I can see that. But not an indiscriminate one." She leaned over to him and whispered in his ear, "You and I have loads in common, Harlan. We're both victims of old men's disputes which have nothing to do with us. But their time is fading, and the future is for the likes of us." She took one of his huge hands between hers. "Let me help you show the world what Harlan Shea can do when he steps out of old man Haxton's shadow."

"What would you have me do?"

"Return what doesn't belong to you, of course."

"You mean rob Haxton."

"I'm just suggesting that together we can end this feud and put things right."

"You'd forgive a man who robbed your mother's grave?"

"I'd forgive a man who's willing to put the past behind him and square up with those he's wronged."

He gazed down at her hands, dwarfed by his own. They were soft, fair, and warm. "What of Alvis O'Connor?"

She dropped his hand back in his lap and walked over to the fireplace, where she stood silently watching the flames for a moment. "Must we talk of him?"

"Does he know I'm here?"

"What if he doesn't?"

"He doesn't, does he? You talked of him this morning like he was the cat's meow. An eastern boy, very educated, very classy, everything an adventurous western beauty could dream of."

She remained quiet.

"But Oswald, he knows I'm here, doesn't he?"

Louisa stared into the fire.

He stood and approached her, gently slid his big, coarse hands up her arms to her shoulders. He brushed her hair away to bare the pale, slender lines of her neck,

- 55 -

and inhaled deeply as faint perfume wafted up from her soft, translucent throat. His strong hands rubbed and massaged the tense muscles of her shoulders and the base of her neck, working their way down her arms. "You two planned for me to come here tonight, didn't you?"

He could feel the tension in her lithe, supple form. Under his strong hands, she felt as though she were on the verge of letting go, almost quivering with the strain of maintaining her stubborn silence.

Finally, she pulled away from him and walked over to the window. "Harlan, you must understand. You weren't bred into this feud, but you walked into it all the same. After mom died, it was just me and Pa. So many long nights he was away, so many days of waiting for him to return, lonely, scared, worried. And we fought, bitterly. I dreaded him when he drank and I hated him for it, for all of it. I wished it would all end. Even if it killed him. Even if it killed me."

"O'Connor must have been a breath of fresh air to you, then."

"Oh, yes, he was. But..." she trailed off.

"But what?"

She paused, thoughtfully. "Perhaps I'm beginning to doubt that there are real differences between men. I'm starting to think the only distinction between saints and sinners is the opportunities luck throws in their path."

"All men must choose, Louisa. Every day we choose to keep the devil inside at bay, or to give up and let loose hell. The end of the former trail is death – poor, tired, and ignoble. But the other trail leads to madness, and there's no turning back once we set a boot down on that road."

"As women, our lot is worse, I think, Harlan. Because we can't make those choices for you."

Shea laughed. "Well, you sure can be persuasive." He put his Stetson on his head and said, "May I come call on you again sometime, Miss?"

"Will you think about my proposition?" Standing in the hotel parlor, Shea proved a mighty intimidating figure. Wide as a steer and so tall he had to bow his head slightly under the door frame, he cast a strikingly rough,

Trouble at Timber Ridge

dark, and threatening form amidst fragile, comfortable things. The old woman who decorated this room with sofas and chairs, doilies, rugs, and delicate lamps never envisioned a visit from the likes of such a man, Louisa decided.

"Louisa, when Lundgren figured out he'd been robbed, he came after us up at Timber Ridge. He shot and killed two close friends of mine, innocent boys who never rode with any gang. He crippled Haxton, and he tried to burn us alive. It was for bringing on that catastrophe that Haxton fired me, and I never denied doing it. Now I'll admit, being robbed like Lundgren was, that's cause for a feud. But to my way of thinking, he's already done plenty to settle the score with Timber Ridge."

She stood thoughtfully looking at him across the parlor and said nothing. Her eyes were moist and her cheeks flushed with emotion.

After a few moments of silence, Shea said, "I'll leave you to your thoughts."

"Must you leave so soon?" Her voice sounded a little desperate.

"It's probably for the best if I go," he said.

He watched her hesitate, conflicted, biting her lip.

When she spoke, her voice was distant, and quivered slightly. "Yes," she said, "it's probably best." She turned her back on him and faced the fire.

He turned down the hall and out the hotel door. When he stepped out of the hotel, it was night. The kerosene lamps were lit, the moon rising. Above his head, the stars gazed down in watchful silence, as distant and disinterested as the ancient gods whose names they bear. He took a deep breath, filling his lungs with the chill, pine-scented air blowing down from the snow-capped mountains. He wondered briefly where Horace had roosted for the night.

Shea was acutely aware of the warm, quiet room behind him. His senses could anticipate the soft caress of a woman's skin pressed against his own, the scent and warmth of her body near him. But he hesitated on the steps only a moment, when somewhere in the distance, a coyote called, mournful and otherworldly. The animal in him urged him on, away from the siren call of woman, away from the comfort and luxury of human companionship, and beckoned him onward, into the untamable darkness, wild and free.

The quiet of the night was shattered by a rifle shot from somewhere hidden in the darkness, followed by a woman's scream.

Chapter 10

"It certainly doesn't reflect well on your alleged innocence that your foreman ran off unexpectedly," Perloe said as he swirled his whiskey in its tumbler and reviewed the facts of the day.

"I don't know what to say," Haxton said. "No idea where the hell he went or why."

"Could be unrelated to the current affair, I suppose," Perloe said, staring at Haxton's expression skeptically over his spectacles. "And then again, it could be your conspirators are beginning to mutiny, now that the eagle eyes of justice have turned upon Haxton Ranch..." He stopped suddenly. "Did you hear that?" he asked, placing his whiskey down on the table.

"Sure did," Haxton said, as he reached for his crutches and both men went out to the yard.

"There he is," Perloe said, pointing at a ranch hand running up from the stables.

"I was ... out in the pasture ... near the overlook," he struggled to catch his breath. "Heard gunshots, coming from town. Rifle. You said ... keep an ear out ... and let you know if—"

"Good man," Haxton said, looking into the darkness in the direction of Timber Ridge. Shea must have uncovered something, he mused. Or someone must be on to him...

At some level, Haxton had been relieved at the detective's arrival. Knowing his own innocence – at least, in the current affair – he hoped the investigation would clear his name with Fairbault, and business could continue as usual. He'd had some trepidation about Perloe turning up evidence of past crimes he had committed, but overall his reaction was one of optimism.

"Town sounds festive tonight," Perloe noted.

Haxton grunted and stomped back inside.

-*- -*- -*-

Wood splintered from the railing just inches from where Shea stood on the hotel steps. Instinctively, he dove behind a horse trough, jerking out his pistols. He fired into the darkness in the direction of the rifle's flash and fading report. Behind him, he heard a scream, and a quick glance up at the hotel window showed Louisa's silhouette.

Suddenly, it struck Shea that she must know something of the shooter's intentions.

"Hold your fire," a voice called from the saloon doorway.

Shea's keen eyes saw a flicker of shadowy movement in the alley between the saloon and the neighboring building where the shots originated. He fired another shot at the movement.

"Hold it, I say!" the voice repeated. When the echoes of his shots died down, he heard running and took off in pursuit.

"Come on, gents, he's on the run," the voice from the saloon yelled, and three or four men took off after Shea.

When Shea got to the end of the alley behind the saloon, he paused, guns at the ready. He peeked around the corner of the building, but there was no sign of life between the backs of the building and the tree line.

Panting men reeking of smoke and liquor caught up to him. "It's Shea, Sheriff," one of them said.

"What's all this shooting about?" the rotund lawman asked.

"Someone took a shot at me from over there as I was walking to my horse," Shea said.

"You ain't been back in town long to start making enemies," Sheriff Reddington said. "Any idea who it was?"

"Maybe," Shea said. "Can't prove nothing, though."

"Shall we search the woods, Sheriff?"

"Dan Waldschmidt, is that you?" Shea asked.

"Welcome back, Harlan," Waldschmidt said. "I see you brought trouble with you. Just like old times."

"Just like old times," Shea agreed.

Trouble at Timber Ridge

"You won't find naught in the wood before it finds you this night," the Sheriff warned. "Best take cover indoors, and perhaps we'll catch him next time."

The group of men trudged back to the street. Shea showed them the pile of barrels and crates where the mysterious shooter had lain in cover. He glanced up at the hotel, and saw Louisa still at the parlor window, staring into the night.

_-*- -*- -*-_

When Waldschmidt stepped back into the saloon, he noticed the conspicuously empty corner table. "Oswald," he muttered to himself.

"What's that?" Reddington asked.

"Nothing, just thinking."

"So, how well do you know this Harlan Shea? He left before I came to town and ran for Sheriff."

"We've known each other for years. Worked together for Haxton. He's a good man."

"Wasn't he fired in disgrace?"

"Everyone makes mistakes."

"If I recall what I've been told correctly, he stole some gold from an outlaw who followed him back to Haxton Ranch and shot the place up. Killed several of the outfit, crippled Haxton, and torched the buildings, ain't that right?"

"Pretty much, that's the story."

"Well if he's a good man, as you say, I'll wager he's bad luck. Won't be staying here long, will he?"

"Don't know. Haxton brought him back to look into some cattle concerns."

"I'm surprised Haxton trusts him, after nearly getting him killed."

"A few years ago, he took down some rustlers the law couldn't catch for stealing stock from Haxton. The Heinz twins – maybe you heard of them."

"Sure, I remember some cowboy caught them after they'd rustled half of Colorado. He was a regular embarrassment to lawmen across the territory, a real blemish to the law's record. So that was him, was it?"

"Yes, that was him."

"And Haxton brought him in 'cause he wants that kind of gunman on his side?"

Dan thought he detected a note of resentment in Reddington's voice. "Reddington, do you know what's going on up there at the ranch?"

"I know it's been a while since I've seen Haxton's outfit drive cattle through town to the depot. I know a few of his boys quit and moved on. And I know Haxton's been something of a recluse of late."

"Ain't you been curious to go up and see Haxton about all this?"

"Haxton don't like me much, and I'd as soon stay clear of him. I've heard tell he's reformed, that it's real and for good in the eyes of the town. But, Shea's been a crook all his life, and when bad times come to men of that sort, it's been my experience they've invited them. Do you trust him?"

"I'd trust him with my life," Waldschmidt said.

"But you admit he's dangerous?"

"I wouldn't sleep well knowing I was on his bad side, I'll give you that."

"Then I'd just as soon he left town," Reddington said. O'Malley came around with a bottle and refilled their drinks. "You'll excuse me, O'Malley, if I note the service is a bit easier on the ol' eyes when it's other than the likes of you."

O'Malley chuckled. "I gave Louisa the night off."

"That O'Connor fella sure is a lucky little runt," Reddington commented. "Almost makes me want to go east and get educated. So, Waldschmidt, you must know something of Shea's friends and enemies then. Any idea who tried to bushwhack him?"

"Well, did you notice where he was comin' from when the shots were fired?"

"Yeah, I suppose he was coming from the hotel. Now that I think of it, wasn't that O'Connor's girl standing in the window?"

"That's where O'Connor's gal is stayin'. And this is her night off."

Trouble at Timber Ridge

"Well, I'll be! Shea, you old dog. But still, I can't imagine O'Connor can hold a rifle straight, or would have the guts to take a shot at a man in cold blood."

"Yeah, especially at a fella who can shoot like Shea. But matters of the heart can do strange things to a feller's reason."

"Reckon I know who I'm looking for then." Reddington slugged back the last drops of red eye, bid Waldschmidt goodnight, and headed out into the street.

Waldschmidt sat for many minutes, deep in thought, swirling the whiskey in his glass. He felt a little guilty putting Sheriff Reddington on the wrong trail, but he needed to buy some time. Finally, Oswald came in, and took his habitual seat at the table. Waldschmidt intentionally made eye contact, and nodded toward the door. Oswald responded with a subtle sneer. Then Waldschmidt stood and walked out into the night, followed after a moment by Oswald.

-*- -*- -*-

After the shots had stopped, O'Connor waited for what he thought was a safe interval before sneaking out of the depot and walking cautiously down the street to investigate. *Probably nothing*, he thought, *just some drunk kid from one of the outfits raising a little hell.* Such foolishness was not unusual in Timber Ridge. The sound of gunfire reminded O'Connor how far he was from St. Louis. He yearned for the comfort and luxury of his father's fine home. He missed a hot breakfast served to him without cost at a comfortable table. He longed to hear music inspired by history and European culture rather than moonshine, and to watch fine ladies stroll about in search of refined husbands with well-fed stomachs stretching tailored suits. Most of all, he resented being immersed in such coarseness, where his intellect seemed of little consequence amid the brutishness of these unpolished, barbaric hill people.

But the St. Louis of his childhood was not all debonair sophisticates with polished shoes. Especially down by the river, or in the evening hours, or in those corners of town where the saloons outnumbered the horse-drawn carriages. There he had been pushed around, even beaten. And while these experiences had left him wary – and not a little jittery – around less cultured folk, something in him yearned to hold that type of power over others.

He sought safety in the shadows, just around the corner of the hotel. Just a few feet from him, though out of sight from his hiding place, was the window of the parlor, the parlor where he visited Louisa, and every thought of Louisa when she was not in his company triggered a pang of jealousy. Louisa attracted a lot of attention from the coarse men of this sleepy little nowhere town, and O'Connor lacked the confidence to trust any woman whom he couldn't keep an eye on at all times.

Briefly, he wondered if she was all right, being in town at O'Malley's so close to where the gunshots had sounded. Then, he wondered if she was at O'Malley's tonight. Or was she in the hotel tonight? Walking over from the depot, he had noticed lights in a few of the rooms upstairs at the hotel. He tried to remember if one of them had been hers. He thought maybe her window had been lit. *Was she expecting someone tonight? Oswald, perhaps?* No, he believed her when she said he made her skin crawl. Oswald made O'Connor's skin crawl too. Could it be that Louisa was receiving other callers? Was this what Oswald hinted at earlier at the depot?

O'Connor reddened beneath the cloak of darkness. Then he heard voices, and instinctively ducked deeper into the shadows. From around the corner of the saloon, the shadows of several men emerged, talking in hushed tones. A few of the men walked up the planks to the saloon door, their boots thunking loudly along the loose boards. But the largest of the shadows made his way alone across the street.

O'Connor pressed himself against the corner of the hotel. The specter neared him, and O'Connor's heart raced as he realized it was walking directly toward him. A dozen memories of shadowy threatening encounters in his childhood revisited him.

Trouble at Timber Ridge

Suddenly, the shadow crossed into the light spilling out of the hotel window, and cast an unnatural, eerie glow on the cool, expressionless face of the man. It was Harlan Shea, and he looked much bigger when he wasn't standing on the safe side of a barred window. And the fact that Shea also made Oswald nervous did nothing to ease O'Connor's discomfort. His mouth felt full of cotton, his legs weak.

Shea stopped six feet from where O'Connor hid and untied the reins of a horse from the hotel hitching post. Shea had not seen him. The gunman had no idea O'Connor lurked there in the shadows. Relieved, O'Connor remained very still and held his breath.

Then, something struck O'Connor. Why was Shea's horse tied outside the hotel instead of O'Malley's Saloon? His little heart sank. Was Shea calling on Louisa? A jealous rage took possession of him. At that moment, Harlan Shea became every man who ever pushed him around. He was every man who made a joke at O'Connor's expense. He was everyone who had ever taken something O'Connor wanted.

O'Connor's heart raced. He'd never fired a gun, but he desperately wanted one then. He pictured himself raising the pistol and drawing a bead on the shadow calmly mounting his horse. He pictured what would happen if he shot Shea from the shadows, unseen, before Shea could draw on him.

Shea's head would jerk. His hat would fall off. His neck would whip to one side. Then the shoulders would slump, and the limp, lifeless body would slide to the ground. Perhaps the horse would rear. Perhaps Shea's foot would be caught in the stirrup when the startled horse took flight. Shea would be dragged until his body was shredded. Harlan Shea, the mythic outlaw, would be dead by O'Connor's hand.

Shea was riding away now, and O'Connor was alone in the shadows again. His fantasy dissolved as quickly as it had formed. He didn't even know how to shoot and, even if he did, he would probably miss. If he missed, Shea would put a bullet in him before he could pull the trigger a second time.

O'Connor stepped out of his hiding place and walked back to the depot, alone with his jealousy and a newly formed hatred of Harlan Shea.

Chapter 11

When Shea rode into the yard at the Haxton Ranch, the telltale, intermittent red glow of a pipe on the porch revealed someone waiting for him. He hitched Delilah and strode to the porch.

"Evenin', boss." he said.

"Pleasant night?" Haxton asked.

"Somebody took a shot at me as I left the hotel."

"The boys heard the shots. Louisa tell you anything?"

"She confirmed that this Oswald fella is bad for business."

"That all?"

Shea paused. "Something on your mind, boss?"

"Johnson's gone."

"When did he leave?"

"You don't sound surprised."

Shea sighed. "I think he's a good man, all in all, but he has his faults."

"Careful, Harlan. You're here for a job. I don't need you protecting people conspiring against me just because you feel sorry for them."

"I'm not protecting anybody, boss."

"You're not exactly being forthcoming, either."

"I don't know the whole story yet."

"Well, you be sure to be straight with me from now on. Is there anything else I should know? Especially, about my own ranch hands?"

"No."

"You sure?"

"Look, boss. I was looking into Johnson, and I turned up some suspicious money down at the bank. I confronted him on it, and he 'fessed up. I was going to fill you in, but I had an engagement with Louisa, so I thought it could wait. I didn't know he was gonna run."

"Next time, you make keeping me in the loop your top priority. Don't you let prancing around town with Louisa get in the way of doing what I hired you for. Now, what about this money at the bank?"

"Johnson didn't know whose it was or where it was going. He was told to make regular withdrawals and give the money to Oswald, who promised to pay down his debt to the Y Bar O outfit."

"Debt?"

"Cards. Seems he didn't know when to quit."

Haxton grunted. "Well, while you were enjoying the company of that beautiful little heartbreaker in town, I spent the evening with a cattle detective."

"What?"

"Sidney Perloe. Seems my buyers sent him to town to investigate me for rustling."

"The blotted brands from the last sale?"

"That's right. He'll be wanting to talk to you too."

"Any particular reason?"

"Just fill him in on what you know."

"Can do."

Haxton got up painfully from his rocker on the porch, tossed his ash in the cold grass with a flick of his pipe, and opened the ranch house door. "I feel like you're holding out on me, Harlan."

"I'm still trying to put it all together, boss. As soon as I figure out something of significance, I'll let you know."

"You'd best do that." With that, Haxton went in and closed the door.

_*_ _*_ _*_

Oswald caught up with Waldschmidt behind the saloon. "You had something to do with this, didn't you, Oswald?" Waldschmidt asked.

"Something to do with what?"

"With the attempt to kill off Harlan Shea."

Oswald smirked. "What makes you think I had anything to do with it?"

Trouble at Timber Ridge

"Look, Oswald, I ain't your partner anymore. We're square, we split the money even, and as I see it I don't owe you nothing."

"No, that's right – we're square."

"I'm an honest man now, Oswald. I'm a small-time rancher with a wife and everything. I ain't got no mind to go back to outlawing, not ever."

"Suit yourself."

"But Harlan Shea is my friend—"

"Stop right there, Waldschmidt. Any issue I've got with Harlan Shea is none of your business."

"It's my business in so far as I don't like my friends getting shot at," Waldschmidt insisted.

"Well, that's where you and I see things differently."

"Know if it comes down to you or Shea, I won't side with you, Oswald."

"That'll be your funeral, Waldschmidt," the dark outlaw replied.

"We both knew this day would come. We both know secrets that could ruin the other, or get him killed. That's been cause enough for a truce – 'til now."

"What are you suggesting?"

"You take another shot at Shea and the truce is off."

Oswald grunted. He didn't like the idea of two skillful gunmen in town being against him. "You realize, Waldschmidt, I could ruin you with just a word to Haxton?"

"Haxton would shoot you dead before you opened your mouth. All I'd have to do is let him know you were there during the shootout years ago, and it would be your death warrant. You think he's forgotten how Lundgren's boys shot up his outfit? How you trapped them for days without food or water? How someone threw a lamp and lit the place ablaze? Exposing my past transgressions would be my chance to call you out in front of your boss. I'm the only reason Haxton survived, so as furious as he would be with me for my part in bringing on that hell, he hasn't forgot I stuck by his side through those days and nights and saved his life in the end."

"All right, Waldschmidt, I hear what you're saying. But after we part company tonight, I'm going to go about my business, and if you get in the way, I'll pump you full of lead."

"Just remember, if I see you draw a bead on Shea, I promise you the same."

Oswald chuckled. "We made quite a team. Too bad you had to go all honest on me. We could have done great things together, you and me."

"That's where you're wrong, Oswald. There's more riches in an honest life than I could have ever stole. It's a shame you can't see that."

Waldschmidt left Oswald mulling over those words in the dark.

-*- -*- -*-

Shea slept surprisingly well again, in spite of his brush with death the night before. He awoke at the sound of a familiar shriek outside in the yard. He stretched and stumbled over to the washstand where he splashed his face with tepid water and dried it on a sleeve. Then, he strapped on his guns, stepped into his boots, and clunked out into the yard.

"That you making all that racket, Horace?" he called at the falcon, who flew readily to the perch offered by Shea's forearm. "Bet there's something for you over in the woodpile." In a singular, lightning-fast motion, Shea whipped out a revolver and fired. The bullet splintered a fair chunk of wood off a pine log and sent field mice scurrying to safety. Horace took flight in a low, straight line to the scurrying mice, picked up two, one after the other in his claws, and flew them up to the roof of the bunkhouse.

"Most remarkable," a man with spectacles said. He stood on the porch smoking a pipe.

"You Perloe?"

"Sidney Perloe, indeed. And you must be the notorious Harlan Shea."

"What the hell's all that shootin' about?" Haxton hollered from inside.

Trouble at Timber Ridge

"Never mind," Perloe called, "all is well out here. Mr. Shea just showed me one of his tricks of falconry."

"You're fond of birds, eh, Perloe?"

"Quite so, quite so. And that peregrine falcon of yours... My word, he must be comparable to the largest specimen on record."

"Horace is a mean old bird. But we've been company for some time, all the same."

"Well, from what I've heard, he's better company than you usually keep."

"What's that now?"

"I have colleagues in Lonsdale, Shea," Perloe said. He removed his spectacles and wiped the lenses with his shirttail. "Quite a few parties would be interested in speaking to you concerning your doings up that way. Now, I don't know all the details, only that the matter is quite unsettled, and the law wishes to speak to you."

"They'll want to do more than speak, I reckon. I assure you, however, I wasn't the first to pull the trigger in Lonsdale. And though I'm not particularly eager to run into them Lonsdale boys again, I got nothing to hide either, Mr. Perloe. I'd as soon forget about it."

"Yes, I'm sure that's true."

"You wanna hold Horace?"

"Who? The falcon? My word, do you think he'd let me?"

"He might. Horace!" Shea raised his arm for a perch, but the bird made no response. "I'm talking to you, dummy. Fly on down here."

Horace looked in Shea's direction, seeming to figure what the cowboy was going on about.

"Come on down, boy. This feller wants to meet you."

Horace squawked indignantly at having his breakfast interrupted, but finally swooped low enough over the stranger's head to make Perloe duck, before circling around to land on Shea's arm.

"Horace, this nice man wants to hold you for a second," Shea said, in a voice somehow both soothing and commanding. Firmly, he held Perloe's coat-clad wrist out parallel to his own, and after a moment, the falcon stepped into Perloe's custody.

"Most remarkable!" Perloe replied.

Shea dug in his pocket for a scrap of dried meat. "Animals ain't much like people, Mr. Perloe," he said, tossing the scrap up to Horace's crooked beak. "If you're nice to them, they tolerate you. If you do them wrong, they raise hell. People, well, as far as I've seen, whether you're nice to them or mean, you never know quite what to expect in return."

Haxton stepped out into the yard. "I see you two have already been introduced. Shea told me after you left last night, Perloe, that he'd confronted Johnson before the latter skipped town."

"I did," Shea said. "Seems your foreman was being blackmailed into some money laundering."

Horace stretched out his wings and flew off to resume his breakfast.

"That so?" asked Perloe, whose attention seemed sluggish in its return from ornithology to the matter at hand. "Who was he working for?"

"He said he didn't know exactly. He was to interact with a man in town whose name keeps coming up as I dig around for information."

"Who's that?"

"Fella named Oswald."

Perloe looked thoughtful. "Can't say I've ever heard of him."

"That's a name I first heard when I was riding on the other side of the law," Haxton admitted. "I never met the fella myself, but he has a reputation for a quick temper and a deficient conscience. Before we parted ways, Lundgren had some business he was concocting with him. Seems like he may still be involved in Lundgren's dirty business."

"The money's in an account in Johnson's name down at the bank," Shea offered.

"Perfectly marvelous!" Perloe said, and it took both Shea and Haxton a moment to realize he was still admiring Horace from afar.

Trouble at Timber Ridge

"Perloe?" Haxton prompted him. "Shall we ride on down to the bank?"

"Whatever for? ... Oh, quite. Well, to the bank tomorrow, then. Today, I'd like a horse to have an inspection of your herds. Shea, I just can't thank you enough. A magnificent specimen."

"My pleasure," Shea replied.

-*- -*- -*-

Shea tied Delilah in front of O'Malley's. It was still early, and few people were up and about. From inside the saloon, he heard raised voices that quickly died down. But it didn't matter. He thought only of breakfast, drawn by the intoxicating scent of bacon and coffee as it wafted through the doorway.

As Shea approached the batwing doors, the voices started again, this time harsh whispers, the sounds of quarrelling people who did not wish to be overheard, punctuated by the occasional clang of tin-ware.

"Wouldn't go in there, if I was you," O'Malley said, as he walked out of the saloon, pipe in hand. "Louisa and her beau are quarrelling again. Bad for business."

"This happen often?" Shea asked.

"Oh, once in a while."

"Any idea why?"

O'Malley looked somewhat affronted. "Harlan, you know I'm no snoop."

"No, of course you're not," Shea said, scratching the stubble on his cheek to conceal a smile. There was another crash inside.

"Well, enough is enough," O'Malley said, dumping his ash and pocketing his pipe. He pushed his way through the doors, and bellowed at the pair. "You two lovebirds, take your spat somewhere else. I've a customer waiting."

A moment later, O'Connor stepped out onto the porch where Shea stood. He jerked to a halt, his startled expression rapidly twisting into a malignant sneer.

"Mornin', O'Connor," Shea said.

O'Connor grunted in response.

Shea had one hand on the batwing doors when he heard O'Connor say behind him.

"A minute, Mr. Shea?" Nervous as he was, there was no hiding the hate in O'Connor's face.

Chapter 12

An autumn chill suggested winter was just around the corner when Perloe and Haxton rode the buckboard down to the bank. As usual, the banker was hunched over his ledger, frantically scribbling away, his nose smudged from frequent scratching with an ink-stained hand.

"Good day, sir," Perloe began. "My name is Sydney Perloe, of Perloe, Watson, and Associates, under the employ of a Mr. Fairbault, cattle buyer and..."

"Sure, I know Fairbault," the banker interrupted, without looking up.

"And with me is Mr. Haxton."

"Never expected to see you set foot in a bank, except maybe to hold it up, Haxton," the banker muttered.

"As tempting as that is," Haxton said gruffly, "we're here to see about an account set up by my foreman Johnson."

"Sure, the one he uses to pay your outfit, presumably?" the banker inquired.

Haxton looked perplexed. Perloe seemed to take note, and continued, "That's right, the one he administers on Mr. Haxton's behalf."

"It's closed," the banker said simply.

"Whatever do you mean?" Perloe asked.

"I mean he cleared it out yesterday, at Mr. Haxton's request." The banker looked up quizzically from his ledger and replaced his pen in its well.

"I see," Perloe said. "Would it be possible to see a record of deposits and withdrawals?"

"I'd be obliged to comply with any legal investigation," the banker said, "as soon as I can verify your credentials."

"Fair business," Perloe replied, and he pulled a letter from his jacket. He also listed several references and their addresses for verification.

"I'll sort through this promptly. Check back in a few days." The banker returned to his scrawling on the ledger.

Haxton slapped a hand down on the banker's desk. "Damn it, it's my money for my outfit. Do it now."

The banker looked up at Haxton, shocked. "All right," he said. "All right. Just give me a minute." He pulled out his ledger and went through a series of line items where withdrawals were recorded. He pointed them out. "They're all the same, as you can see," the banker said. "Each is on the day your men were to be paid. The only exception, of course, is the last withdrawal, just yesterday, when the account was emptied and closed."

"Perloe, I'm flummoxed." Haxton pronounced, exasperated, as they stepped out into the street. "I never had Johnson set up any account, and my boys haven't been paid in months."

"Haxton, it doesn't look good. A bank account connected to your name with money that never made it to your outfit, and suddenly I show up and it's empty. You must see this appears quite damning." Perloe looked at Haxton with something like sympathy. "Yet, my gut tells me you're being sincere about all this. No offense meant, but you don't seem the type of man likely to set up so elaborate a deception."

"No offense taken."

"If I recall correctly, there was a time when if you wanted to make off with funds, you simply applied a bit of gunplay, and were on your way."

"In some ways things were sure simpler then."

"I'm beginning to suspect you're being in some way set up. I've reviewed your stock and I've found nothing but pure and beautifully branded cattle. I've gone over your books, and there is nothing out of sorts. But this business with the bank account and Johnson's sudden disappearance makes me wonder if he was conspiring to paint you as a rustler."

Trouble at Timber Ridge

"I have a hard time believing Johnson would do that. He's young, a hard worker, and we got on fine."

"Yes, well perhaps he was compelled to participate, by threat or by greed. Nevertheless, the question remains, who is the puppeteer holding Johnson's strings? And what motivation would such an individual have to mar your reformed reputation?"

"Well," Haxton began, "I'm not without enemies, I'll give you that. I've wronged a fair number of men in my former days. But there is one in particular who comes to mind."

_*_ _*_ _*_

Shea turned to face O'Connor on the porch of O'Malley's. "What's on your mind, O'Connor?"

"I want you to stay away from her," O'Connor stammered.

"Is that what this is about, O'Connor?" Shea asked. "You think I'm after your girl?"

"I know you called on her the other night over at the hotel."

Shea thought there was a little choke in the telegrapher's voice, and he felt a little sorry for him. "She asked me over for a little chat. It was all business, though it was none of yours," Shea said.

Suddenly, there was a shriek from just behind O'Connor, an inhuman cry. O'Connor's nerves could hold on no longer. He let out a scream and spun around. On the railing behind him perched Horace, watching with evil little eyes.

Shea laughed, and O'Connor reddened.

Perloe and Haxton strolled up. Haxton covered his mouth and faked a cough to cover his snickering. But Perloe's eyes were fixed on the large falcon perched on the rail. "Why, every time I see that remarkable falcon, I'm struck that it must be a giant of its species," he said.

Horace shrieked eerily.

"Don't suppose you've come back here to see the pretty little miss again." Haxton hauled his bum leg up the step toward Shea. "Remember what I said, Harlan. A girl like that's prone to make a man forget his priorities."

"That's my girl you're talking about," O'Connor said.

Haxton ignored him. "She'll have you purring in her lap when you should be hunting down whoever's doin' me wrong." Haxton limped up the stairs and into the saloon, Perloe at his side.

"Shea, I want you to keep away from her," O'Connor repeated.

"You still here?" Shea said, and turned to enter the saloon. When he did, he found Louisa sitting hunched over a table, staring thoughtfully at the wall. A cleaning rag lay crumpled on the table in front of her. The air was still, cool, and rich with the smell of coffee, bacon, and biscuits.

Haxton and Perloe sat across the room, and were conversing with O'Malley.

"Seems business is slow this morning," Shea said.

She looked up at him, a questioning look in her wet, reddened eyes. "Huh? Oh, well, yes it is." She sighed deeply. "Alvis and I had another quarrel. It was humiliating."

"You're lucky he keeps you on after a scene like that."

"Well, sometimes I wish he'd let me go and I could get the hell out of this damned town once and for all." She reddened at her own language. "I'm sorry, it's ... it's just that Alvis asked me to do something I just can't do."

Shea felt an instant rise in his blood pressure. "You mean to run off with him?"

"No. I mean, yes, that too. But something else as well."

Shea was silent for a minute, waiting to see if she would disclose more. When she did not, he prompted her, "Well, what then?"

She gave him an odd look. "It's one thing, Harlan, to avenge your father. It's quite another to rob a stranger."

"O'Connor is getting greedy, is he?"

"Oswald has a tight hold on him. I think that has as much to do with it as anything."

"And your little scheme has been so successful he wants to apply it to someone else."

"Oswald has a new enemy in this town, it seems. Now he wants a little revenge of his own."

Trouble at Timber Ridge

"On Dan Waldschmidt?"

Louisa stood up so quickly she knocked over the chair. "How did you know?"

"Just a hunch."

Louisa looked at him in wonder. Large doe eyes seemed to stare through him, to search the dark and dusty corners of his soul. He wanted to gather her up and hold her on his lap, smell her hair and kiss her. This image was laughable. In spite of her inner strength and fighting spirit, she was dainty next to him, and the intimacy he imagined was as ridiculous as a princess cuddling with a grizzly. Besides, that a girl he had only met a few times could impress him so powerfully unnerved him; it was an unknown experience to him. He had known many girls, but those had been fleeting associations by choice and left him without regret. Moreover, in times he'd sought the companionship of the gentler sex, they typically involved matters of expediency and deception. Once he'd sought a widow's embrace as she hid him from a posse. Another time, he played the fool for a Mormon girl while a vicious storm ravaged the plains. A farmer's daughter, enticed to risk by boredom and drunk with the excitement of consorting with an outlaw, had sheltered and pleasured him in the musty hay of a dilapidated barn. But this girl was different. He had no desire to deceive Louisa and felt an overpowering urge to protect and comfort her.

"Harlan, you know why I'm here – what I was intended to do. I came here to get Alvis in my father's employ by batting my eyelids and wiggling my hips. I did my father's job well, too well apparently."

"Do you love O'Connor?"

"Maybe. I don't know. I think I was starting to. Perhaps I could."

"Would you marry him?"

"Would I marry him? Oh, God, Harlan, I don't know. I wish I hadn't brought this up." She looked thoughtful for a moment. "I could go back to Pa."

"Your Pa's worse for you than O'Connor, Louisa. You know that. There are men on both sides of the law out to kill your Pa. O'Connor at least has honest work, and still has his reputation."

"Not if he's conspiring to rob Dan. Helping avenge one man is one thing, but indiscriminate robbery is quite another."

"You need to tell Waldschmidt – for your conscience's sake."

"How can I betray my own father, Harlan, whatever type of man he is? Or my ... or Alvis? No matter what I've come to think of either of them, how could I live with myself? I knew what I was getting into when I came up here. I planned to seduce a telegraph officer and defraud a rancher. And look what a job I've done! I'm perfectly willing to reap what I've sown, but I can't turn on Pa and Alvis for the same crimes I'm complicit in."

"Then I'll save you the trouble," Shea said, and without waiting for her to reply, he turned and left the saloon.

"What? No, wait, Harlan. Please..." But he was gone, all thoughts of breakfast forgotten.

As Shea stepped out onto the porch of the saloon, a voice off to the side of the porch said, "Shea."

Shea turned, and found himself face to face with O'Connor. The telegrapher looked shaky, and a bead of sweat ran down his temple. "I need to talk to you."

"Wouldn't mind a word with you, myself."

O'Connor gulped. "Around the corner – the alley – where we can talk in private."

"Fine," Shea said. He turned his back and marched across the porch and around the corner into the alley beside the saloon. O'Connor followed.

Shea stopped, some dozen paces into the narrow alley. Then, he turned to face O'Connor, and found himself looking down the barrel of a pistol. The gun visibly shook as the hand holding it trembled. But it was just a couple feet from Shea's face, a distance so close that no one could miss.

"I could do it, Harlan Shea," O'Connor muttered through locked teeth. His voice was strained, breaking. "I could squeeze this trigger right now and kill you."

Trouble at Timber Ridge

Shea smiled. O'Connor was scared to death. "And suppose you did. What then? Do you think that slender neck of yours could just slip through the rope?"

"I could run," O'Connor said, uncertainty furrowing his brow.

"That might help," Shea said. "But there'd be men running after you. Men who've killed before. Put the gun down, O'Connor. You're not ready to kill anybody, and you're not cut out for the life of an outlaw. It's not as easy or as glamorous as you've read. It's a lonely life of never trusting anyone, sleeping with one eye open, and knowing that at some point somebody's going to stick a knife in your back or put a bullet through your liver."

Shea took a step closer to O'Connor, whose hand quivered. He heard Horace's concerned screech from the roof corner.

Then, Shea noticed O'Connor's gaze flicker to something behind him. He clawed at his gun in its holster, but it was too late. A pistol butt came down on his head, and his vision darkened. He was dimly aware of a large stranger, nearly Shea's equal in height if not bulk, hauling him behind the saloon where a few horses were tied to a stump. He made out the vague shape of a falcon circling high above them, and then lost consciousness.

Chapter 13

Soon after his failed attempt to kill Shea, Oswald learned of Johnson's flight. He had given orders to Henry, a large, imposing underling from White Pines ranch, to take care of Shea. "Take him alive, Henry," Oswald instructed. "He's mine. I want credit for settling the score with Harlan Shea." Then, he'd turned his back on the town and taken up Johnson's trail.

He knew Johnson would not try to ride over the mountains. Winter was coming on, and he hadn't the toughness to conquer the high, lonely passes. Except for the cold dew, it had been dry, and the hoof prints in the dust had preserved well. The way Oswald figured it, there was plenty of commerce between the bank and town, but traffic between the bank and the southern road was rare. Sure enough, there was only one set of prints heading south. Oswald followed, figuring he was a day or two behind Johnson.

The ground leveled into the plains, and the wind was an unforgiving blast of cold air. It battered horse, rider, and land alike with the callous playfulness a cat reserves for a mouse. The dust on the trail blew about, and prints became scarce. Oswald was sure Johnson never counted on being followed. The spacing of the prints until Oswald lost them showed the relaxed gate of a rider who was either enjoying his ride or saving his horse.

The stony foothills left behind, visibility was fine for Oswald on the dirt road across the tall grass prairie. The stiff, brown grasses had yet to be crushed flat under the snows of winter. Stalks of dead black-eyed Susans stood tall and proud, holding their dark orbs to the sky in defiance of the coming winter. Heavy gray clouds rolled

Trouble at Timber Ridge

slowly across the sky, promising snow or freezing rain somewhere ahead.

Every few miles, Oswald's experienced eyes would detect signs that his quarry passed this way. At one point, he happened upon the cold embers of a campfire. A little later, he came upon the bones of a jackrabbit, picked clean. Early on the second evening of his hunt, Oswald saw the smoke of a campfire just beyond a bluff. He hobbled his horse, removed a lariat, and crept slowly through the dead grasses.

Fortune favored Oswald. The wind blew into his face, such that his scent did not blow into the sensitive nostrils of Johnson's horse.

Suddenly, Johnson stood and whirled around.

Soon, Oswald could hear it too – a lone voice singing in the wind, distant and hauntingly familiar. The sound dissolved until Oswald was uncertain whether it had been there at all.

Oswald maintained his vigil for a few minutes.

Johnson calmed and retired to his seat at the fire.

The hunter resumed his stealthy approach. Soon his fingers jammed painfully against something half sunken in the soil. It felt rough, but its shape indicated the object was man-made. He traced an arc and realized he'd found a wagon wheel. Then Oswald's eyes spotted irregularities in the ground, oblong mounds low to the ground. *Graves*, he thought, *but who buried these people here?*

He crept onward, but was still farther away than he liked to get a sure shot at Johnson. Again, his hands came in contact with a smooth irregularity in the ground. This one, though, was porous and easily shook free. A human skull, which was not surprising considering the graves. He rolled the skull aside and out of his way then wiped his hand on his trousers. A cold, icy shudder rolled up his spine, and he felt the hairs on his neck stand up. This was a place tainted with death in a way that even the least superstitious would shun. Oswald would be happy to be free of it.

Johnson felt it too, Oswald realized as he watched him. Johnson soon rose to his feet again, staring into the darkness, pistol drawn. There was movement on the other side of the campfire, although Oswald could not make it out at first. Then, a large, dark, and nebulous form – too tall to be a man – moved closer and closer to Johnson. Oswald felt a lump in his throat. He gripped his revolver tightly.

A rider dismounted, a dark form stepping into the firelight. "Those beans I smell, stranger?" the rider asked. "Mind if I share your fire for a spell? It's turning damned cold."

Johnson holstered his pistol. "Sure, be my guest."

Oswald stared in amazement. The rider was Gust Lundgren. Oswald rubbed his eyes and looked again. *Well*, he thought, *I shouldn't be surprised.* This was the main road between this part of Colorado and the site of Lundgren's White Pines ranch and hideout in Texas. He drew his gun and kept it trained on Johnson as he rose and walked into the firelight.

"Oswald? What the hell are you doing out here?"

"What am I doing out here?" Oswald laughed. "I've been tracking this fella for two days! Johnson, put your gun down, you're covered from both sides."

"Whatever for?" Lundgren asked.

Oswald laughed again, a wicked sound, like a banshee cry in the black wind. "This here is Johnson."

"Johnson?" Lundgren's surprise was as great as Oswald's. "Fella who's supposed to be making the withdrawals?"

"The same. And boss, the only reason I knowed he left town was that I caught wind he'd done a fine job of withdrawing the very last cent."

"That so?"

"Look, if it's the money you want, it's on my horse. Take it, and you'll never see the likes of me again, I swear."

"Damned right, I'll never see the likes of you again. Oswald, check his horse. You, boy, put your gun down."

"Not until I'm good and clear out of here."

Oswald called from behind Johnson, "It's here, boss, damned near all of it."

Trouble at Timber Ridge

"Good," said Lundgren, and he shot Johnson in the abdomen. The former foreman of Timber Ridge stumbled back and fell nearly at Oswald's feet. Johnson's horse danced, startled. "Now bring that sack over here to me. I want my just wages."

Oswald, reflecting on how uncomfortable his boss could make him at times, stepped over Johnson and near the fire to hand the money to Lundgren. "Didn't know you was coming, boss."

"Looks like it's a good thing I did. Damn it, Oswald, I trusted you could handle this thing on your own. I figured I'd get up here, surprise you, and find everything running just as planned."

"I was handling it..."

"You were chasing a runaway across the prairie when God knows what the telegraph officer is up to. Probably quaking in his boots and thinking of running himself."

Oswald started to lose his grip on his temper. This was all a waste of time, he knew. The excessively convoluted revenge scheme was beginning to fall apart around them and the risk to his own neck was increasing. But worst of all, in his view, was that every minute he spent away from White Pines was a minute wasted. None of this could serve Oswald's own purpose in the slightest. What he needed was time to spend with pick and torch, crawling about in the darkness, searching for the loot hidden there. If he could uncover just one more stash like the one he and his partner unearthed before, he would be set for life. He could put the West behind him and satisfy all his appetites until he died happily of his excesses.

"Well, if you ask me," he muttered in a low, half-hearted voice, "this whole plan of yours stinks. Why don't you just let me knife Haxton in his bed and be done with it?"

Lundgren glowered at his henchman's insubordination. He stayed silent for nearly a full minute, his evil eyes boring into Oswald, sending chills up the younger man's spine. Finally, Lundgren said, "Oswald, when I put the bullet in Haxton's hip, I was madder than hell that I'd missed. There's nothing so damnably infuriating as being on the verge of revenge only to have the moment of triumph wrenched from your hands. But as the years passed, I began to realize fate offered me an opportunity for a more refined, less merciful revenge than murder could ever offer. Just think, Oswald, what happens to a rancher who can't sell a cow?"

"He goes hungry."

"And he gets desperate."

Oswald thought a moment. "You trying to make an outlaw of Haxton again?"

"That's the thing, Oswald. His riding days are done on account of my bullet. If he can't be an honest rancher, and he can't ride with a gang, he's got nothing left but an empty belly and diminishing funds. He'll gradually watch the outfit quit, the cattle die, the ranch go to the bank. He'll be destitute and powerless to redeem himself. I don't plan to kill him, Oswald. I plan to make him suffer a long, slow, agonizing destruction. But there's just one problem. You're here."

"So that's why you wanted Fairbault to send in a cattle detective. Well, don't worry about O'Connor; he won't be going anywhere. Not without Louisa, anyway."

"How do you mean?"

"He's been begging her to elope."

"Is he now?" There was hell in his voice and whiskey on his breath.

Oswald swallowed hard. "And Harlan Shea's back in town."

"Harlan Shea? What the hell's he up to? Tell me he's not come back to work for Haxton!"

"I've handled him, it'll be fine. I left Henry with orders to take him out of the picture."

"Well, I bet if there's any man who can take down Shea, it's Henry."

Oswald was happy the darkness veiled his blush.

"Dumb as a mule, but in size and strength, he's 'bout Shea's equal. But I don't want him killed, Oswald. Not yet. Not until I make him my offer."

"You're not still thinking about hiring..."

Trouble at Timber Ridge

"Sure I am."

"But he's working for Haxton!"

"That'll just make revenge sweeter. But not if it costs me my daughter."

"Boss, I swear, I kept my eye on her. I followed her best I could manage, keeping out of sight. When a couple times she caught me, she turned all wildcat on me. But I couldn't be with her all the time, could I?" Oswald swallowed hard, then continued, "I followed her when she went to visit the doctor. That was, well, about when Shea arrived. I listened under the window. I could only hear bits and pieces, you know, but I ... I heard..."

"Out with it, Oswald. What did you hear?"

"She's in the family way, boss."

Lundgren stood for a long moment in stunned silence. Then, his face slowly shifted to rage. "Dammit, I swear I'll tear the little bastard apart, see if I don't. As for you, I'll deal with you – what the devil?" A horse, with a rider slumped over its back, thundered into the night, interrupting Lundgren.

Oswald spun and looked. "Johnson's tougher than I would have thought. I'll go after him."

"To hell with him, he won't ride long with my bullet in him. You get back to Henry quick as you can, and be sure he doesn't kill Shea before I deliver my proposition. I'll head into town and fix O'Connor's notions about my daughter."

Chapter 14

Darkness had settled over Timber Ridge. There was a chill in the air, and gusts of wind whistled as drafts penetrated the house, causing miniature cyclones of dust and ash around the floor. Perloe appeared deep in thought, a fact made clear by the unusually long duration since he made his last irrelevant observation about local birds. He stared piercingly at the grain of the table, in uncomfortable silence.

Haxton cleared his throat awkwardly. "Still think I'm a rustler, Mr. Perloe?"

"If you are," the old detective muttered without looking up, "you're either too good to be caught or too dumb to be successful ... I say, none of this makes sense. As best I can figure after the interview with the banker this morning, someone's selling rustled cattle in your name and then paying your foreman the profits. Clearly, he's been bought off. One man couldn't pull this off on his own, at least not while working full time for you. It would be a very clever cover-up indeed if you were behind it, but for one obvious fact."

"You mean that it's costing me money instead of making me money?"

"Well, yes, that is precisely it. It is at the expense of your good name, and directly interfering with your honest sales. You are bleeding funds, I can tell. Your men are unpaid and quitting. And this whiskey – you've watered it down."

Haxton reddened in admission.

"Sorry, I didn't mean to cause you any embarrassment. I'm just enumerating several facts which seem to challenge any motive you might have to rustle yourself. I have the sense I need to focus on how this was pulled off, and that may lead me to some clues about who

Trouble at Timber Ridge

was behind it. I have a mind to go down to the telegraph office and query the agent there."

Haxton harrumphed. "Good luck with that. Shea says he's about as pleasant and personable as a mule. He's been down to check him out several times. Says O'Connor's shut up tight as a clam now. He's on the defensive and he ain't talkin'."

Perloe stared out at the dark for a while and sipped his diluted whiskey. "You seem to think highly of Shea."

"I do."

"He has your trust?"

"Completely."

"A lot of the law want to bring him in, you know."

"So you've said. He kill somebody?"

"A few. One victim was the sheriff of the town Shea was looking for work in. Popular man."

"I wouldn't have figured Shea for killing a lawman."

"Well, that's just the thing. He was a crooked lawman. The cattlemen had a tight hold on the town, ran it with an iron fist, and they used the sheriff to exert their control. Folks who opposed them started to disappear. Shea was a stranger, came to town looking hungry and seeking out a job on the line. He started getting friendly with some of the townsfolk, shop clerks, and such who were pretty regular put out by the cattlemen. The owner of the general store, fella who was outspoken about the abuses of the cattlemen, got himself elected mayor. When he disappeared, Shea took the law into his own hands. Sheriff, two ranchers, and a few cowboys were sleeping underground before Shea hit the trail. They've been combing the countryside for him ever since."

-*- -*- -*-

When Johnson was a boy on his father's modest ranch in Texas, his father did a fair bit of business with Mexicans and traveled across the border from time to time. Mr. Johnson liked to bring back trinkets for Johnson and his older brother. Once, he brought back a small scrap of leather, etched and painted with a picture of a skeleton riding a skeleton horse, some token from a Dia de los Muertos celebration. When Mr. Johnson died,

Johnson's older brother inherited the ranch, and Johnson kept most of the trinkets.

As he careened across the prairie, using up all his fading strength to keep from tumbling off the neck of his horse, his weakening mind kept recalling the skeleton man on the skeleton horse. Johnson knew he was dying, and hoped he had time to get back to town. Now that he knew he had been a pawn in Lundgren's plan for revenge on Haxton, he could think only of using his dying breath to warn the rancher he unknowingly betrayed.

The wicked wind whispered discouragement in his ears, and the cold, distant stars watched apathetically from above. Johnson clung to the neck of the horse with his right arm, while he hung limp and bloody in his saddle. Periodically, he raised his head and peered through the dark behind him, certain he would be pursued. But the blackness revealed nothing. So he clung desperately to life and saddle, urging his mount to ever greater speed.

-*- -*- -*-

When Shea awoke, he found himself in a small derelict cabin. He had no idea how long he'd been unconscious, but it was dawn and getting lighter. His head throbbed, and he sat for what seemed hours while consciousness fully returned and the world around him stopped spinning. His ribs hurt on one side, a bruise from the pommel of a saddle, he figured. They probably laid him across a horse and carried him out of town. But where was he?

"Well, look who's waking up from his beauty sleep," Oswald said, standing in the doorway while smoking a cigarette. He'd spent most of the night on a horse making for the abandoned cabin he and Henry had been using as a hideout and base of operations.

Shea had no idea who the other man was, though he figured he was the one who attacked him and brought him here. Shea realized he was tied to an old chair that creaked as he tested his arms against the bonds. He'd been tied effectively, his hands down at his sides.

Oswald eyed his captive with disdain.

Chapter 15

Louisa was sweeping the dust off the porch in front of O'Malley's when she saw a horse, apparently riderless, trotting across the tracks and into town. At first she thought the horse must have escaped a corral, but this animal seemed to move with a deliberation uncharacteristic of a wild horse. As the animal neared, she realized there was a rider slumped in the saddle. She bolted, racing into the street to catch the reins.

Louisa hitched the reins to the post in front of O'Malleys, and struggled to free the man from the stirrups. Pulling his limp form from the horse's back, she learned he weighed more than he appeared and she was not as strong as she thought. Both rider and woman tumbled to the cold, hard ground. As she pushed herself up, she realized it was Bryce Johnson, Haxton's ranch foreman. His face pallid and lips colorless, his eyelids were only half-open. His breath sounded strained. She felt his pulse, and it raced. But he did seem to be responding to her a little.

"Wake up," she said. "Try to stay awake. I'll run and get the doctor."

"No, no," Johnson said. "Too late... Stay with me. Please."

She cradled the dying man's head in her lap.

He looked up into her eyes and said, "I know you."

"Of course. I'm Louisa, I've served you at O'Malley's."

"No, I mean I know who you are. You're..." He choked and coughed up spittle tainted with blood, but was too weak to wipe it away. "You're Gust Lundgren's daughter."

"How? How do you know that?"

"I didn't know ... before. I didn't know I was working for your father. I didn't know until he shot me."

Louisa felt ill, physically and spiritually. "Pa? Pa shot you? I'm sorry ... I never knew this would..."

"No, please. Let me finish. I don't have much time. Haxton, he was good to me. Took me under his wing. Gave me a good job and his trust. I betrayed him. I didn't know, but I did. Tell him. Please, tell him I'm sorry. Tell him I tried to make it back to tell him myself. Tell him ... I tried."

"I'm going to get the doctor. Please, hold on. Stay with me."

"Tell him I tried..." Johnson said. His breathing began to slow. In moments it stopped.

Louisa sat in the dust, holding the dead man's head tenderly in her lap as his blood cooled. Passersby gathered in a tight little circle around the scene. Someone placed a hand on her shoulder. Looking up through tearful eyes, she saw O'Malley. This was it, this was the end of her complicity in her father's plans, she decided. This poor man, just a boy really, who had been drawn into this feud against his will was an innocent victim of violence in her eyes. In her mind, she saw her father for what he was – a cold, calculating killer who would destroy anything and everyone in his path who crossed him. Every blow he had ever struck her, every harsh word he'd ever spoken, came flooding back to her. And she hated him. She hated him with all her heart and soul. "It took this poor boy's life to show me Pa for what he was," Louisa muttered to herself. Then, she wept.

_-*- -*- -*-_

Oswald strode across the cabin to the chair where Shea was bound, and spat in his face. "You sure you got the right guy here, Henry? This fella don't look so dangerous. Just looks like an unemployed cowpuncher who's come back to town to beg for his meat."

Henry chuckled from the doorway where he stood and leaned his shotgun against the doorframe.

Oswald kissed his knuckles and punched Shea on the cheek. The force of the blow nearly knocked him over. "You're lucky. The boss wants you alive. He wants to talk to you about something. I was gonna have Henry save

Trouble at Timber Ridge

you so as I could look you in the eyes while I killed you, but that will have to wait. But, mark my words, your days are numbered. And as soon as the boss tires of you, well, let's just say I'm looking forward to it."

Oswald turned, and started to walk out of the cabin, but paused just a moment at the door. "Oh, and I hope you had fun with Louisa while it lasted," he said. "Can't imagine there's much of a future for you and her now, what with O'Connor's baby in her belly." He stepped out of the cabin, laughing.

Shea's face contorted to rage.

Henry stepped out of the cabin with Oswald. "You going someplace?" he asked.

"Boss is seein' red. I'll wager he's on his way to deal with O'Connor right now. I figure it's all over, the whole affair. We won't be here much longer." Oswald chuckled. "Can't wait to kick the dust of this damn place off my boots. I'm gonna lay low 'til the dust settles – I suggest you do the same."

"Fine business. I can keep an eye on him, boss. In that condition, at least."

A few seconds later, Shea began to hum.

Henry's shadow obscured the doorway. "What did you say?" he asked.

"Didn't say nothing," Shea said.

"Then what's that I heard?"

"This?" Shea started humming again. A haunting tune, something he didn't remember where he'd first heard it.

"You knock that off," Henry said.

Shea leaned forward in his chair, and found he could stand with the four legs of the chair fully off the floor of the cabin. "

"What the hell are you doing?" Henry demanded, reaching for the shotgun.

Shea kept humming, then with shocking quickness, he threw his mighty weight against the back wall of the cabin, shattering the chair. The limp ropes fell in a pile at his feet. His right hand caught the chair's back spindle.

The suddenness shocked Henry and he hesitated a moment, taking a step back into the doorframe of the cabin. Then he snatched up the shotgun and whipped it around, pointing at Shea's vitals.

Shea was a few paces shy of being able to clobber Henry with the spindle. He started to hum again.

"You hum another note and I'll blow your head apart," Henry said.

"All right, I'll quit," Shea said. "As for you, whatever you do, don't turn around."

"What?" Henry said, glancing over his shoulder through the doorway.

There was an angry flutter of wings, and a high-pitched shriek. Hard, razor sharp talons tore at Henry's eyes and face, shredding his visage to bloody ribbons.

Henry screamed.

Then Shea brought the spindle down hard on the back of the blinded man's head. "I told you not to turn around," Shea said. "Good to see you, Horace," Shea said, his voice all but drowned out by the screams of the bleeding man writhing across the threshold.

Shea leapt on one of the horses and tore off down the trail. "Hurry, girl," he said, "or that O'Connor runt is wolf bait." Far above his head, came the eerie shriek of the soaring falcon. *Alvis O'Connor is a pain in the rump*, Shea thought. *But, dammit, Lundgren, it ain't right makin' a young tenderfoot do your dirty work for you one minute and blowing a hole through him the next. And it sure ain't right using your daughter's charms to turn an innocent young man into a criminal.*

As they broke free of the tree line, Shea pushed the horse to the utmost.

_*_ _*_ _*_

Mary Waldschmidt was content to keep to herself and rarely had company. "Dan," Mary called to her husband as he rode into the yard. "Come on in, Dan. There's a girl here to see you."

Confused, Waldschmidt pulled up quickly and dismounted. "What's this all about, then?" he asked, stepping into the kitchen. A beautiful young woman sat

Trouble at Timber Ridge

at the kitchen table, fear and resolve in her red-rimmed blue eyes.

"Dan, this is Louisa," Mary said.

"We've met, down at O'Malley's," Dan said, blushing.

"Pleased to meet you, formally," Louisa said, extending her hand, which he took. Despite the tears staining her face, she was a portrait of beauty and misery. With a quiver in her throat, she added, "My real name is Louisa Lundgren."

"Lundgren!" Dan said, spitting out the name. "As in Gust Lundgren?"

"My father," Louisa softly admitted. Her legs were weak, trembling, so she remained seated.

"Your father tried to kill my former employer," Dan started.

"Easy, Dan," Mary said. "Let the girl talk."

"You threw yourself on his gun," Louisa said. "Pa told me. Knocked off his aim so he only managed to shoot Mr. Haxton in the hip."

"He never rode again after that," Dan said through gritted teeth.

"Pa said what you did was the bravest, most loyal thing he'd ever witnessed. Pa admires courage, even in those who stand up to him." She swallowed. "Pa admires virtue in others, even though he has little of his own."

Dan's blood began to cool. He took a seat opposite Louisa and accepted a cup of coffee from Mary. "Well, what are you here for?"

She swallowed, and struggled to compose herself. "Oswald and Alvis are planning to cheat you."

"What? Cheat me? What the devil do you mean?"

"Alvis has been redirecting telegrams between you and Haxton and your buyers. He's been turning them over to Oswald and Pa. They know you're planning to sell out and move on. He responded to the buyers that the first shipment of cattle is imminent. Only he plans for the shipment to arrive from White Pines, not from Timber Ridge. It's a chance for them to sell a lot of cattle they've rustled in Texas, all at once, by doing it in your good name." She said the last part with her eyes closed, as though she worried she would not be able to finish this confession if she witnessed its effect on the Waldschmidts.

Dan sat in stunned silence. "But it will never work. The buyers will see the brands are different on the cattle coming in."

"Pa's outfit is pretty experienced at blotting brands."

Dan's fist hit the table, and the girl jumped.

Mary was over in an instant, a cooling hand on her husband's shoulder, but her words directed to Louisa. "So he's selling his stolen cattle off by impersonating honest ranchers in telegram messages. Has he told you all this, or did you figure it out?"

She swallowed back a sob. "I've helped him."

Dan stared at her.

"Pa sent me to Timber Ridge under the name of Campbell. He heard a young man from St. Louis had come set up a telegraph station at the depot in town. He told me to make him fall in love with me. Then, I was to convince him to divert telegrams coming to and out of Timber Ridge as best served Pa's plans."

"Has the shipment already gone north, do you know?"

"No, I think there's still time to stop it."

Dan rose to his feet. "Good," he said. "I'll ride down to see the sheriff. He'll know how to fix all this. And I'll see that the little crook of a telegrapher ends up behind bars."

"Dan, wait," Mary said. "Go on, dear, tell him the rest of it."

"Alvis, he wants me to elope with him. He's scared of Pa, and he knows there's trouble in the wind. But he's not practical, and he'll have a tainted reputation. There won't be anywhere in Colorado he can get work as a telegrapher after this, and there's ... there's..." She choked back her tears.

"And there's a baby coming," Mary said, softly.

Dan sat there in thought. "I see," he almost whispered.

After a moment, Louisa continued in a voice controlled only by great effort. "Alvis has no idea how he'll

Trouble at Timber Ridge

be able to provide for me, let alone a baby. His only thought is running. I'm scared to death of what Pa will do to Alvis when he finds out. He gets crazy when he's angry."

"Louisa could stay with us, Dan," Mary said. "I can look after her, until the baby comes."

Dan hesitated.

Louisa shook her head. "No, I couldn't do that."

"Mary's right," Dan said. "You might be better off with us, at least 'til O'Connor finds work."

"He's not likely to find work behind bars, which is where he'll be if he sticks around here much longer," Louisa said. "You two have been far too kind when by all rights you ought to hate me. It's just too much for me to ask."

Mary says, "You haven't asked. We've offered."

Still weeping, Louisa rose. "No, you've been kind enough."

The Waldschmidts escorted her to the door and watched Louisa make her way back toward town. Dan called out after her, "Come on back if you change your mind."

"What do you think Mr. Lundgren will do when he finds out, Dan?" Mary asked.

"Reckon it will be ugly," Dan said. "She's pretty well signed her father's death warrant, whether she realizes it or not, by what she's admitted to being involved in."

"But, Dan, you won't get involved in all this, will you?"

"Not beyond ensuring that our sale goes through. But Haxton's called a man in to sort out some trouble he's been having with his buyers. He didn't let on to the nature of the trouble, but now that Louisa confessed, I think I can put two and two together."

"Who's the man, a lawman?"

"Harlan Shea."

"The gunfighter? Oh Dan, please stay out of this. Please don't get involved!"

"I'll have Sheriff Reddington keep it as discrete as possible. I'll sort out our sale, and try to get out of the way before all hell breaks loose." He reached for his coat.

"Dan?"

"Yes?"

Mary looked at her husband thoughtfully. "It sure would be nice to finally hear a baby in the house, wouldn't it?"

Chapter 16

The depot manager was sleeping off his liquor again. O'Connor stayed so busy with train orders and the incessant chatter of commerce that he didn't even look up when the depot door opened. Heavy boots with spurs clunked and jangled across the creaky boards of the waiting room.

"Be with you shortly," he called without looking up from the small desk pressed up against the wall of the tightly cramped office. A moment later, there was a crash and a splintering of wood as two hundred pounds smashed open the door like it was a child's toy. O'Connor tried to scramble to his feet, but fell over his chair, and sprawled across the floor.

Lundgren appeared, an imposing figure in the doorway. O'Connor felt Lundgren looming right on top of him.

"Didn't Oswald warn you, boy," Lundgren snarled, "not to get no funny ideas about my daughter?"

O'Connor scrambled to his feet, and stood nervously, hardly daring to glance at Lundgren. "I been nothin' but kind to her, sir, I swear!"

"Oswald says otherwise." He stepped into the room, and O'Connor took another step back.

"I swear! I've been up to nothing other than seeing through your plan..."

"Like hell. Johnson's tried to run off with the cash. What's worse, Oswald says the cattle detective's gettin' mighty chummy with Harlan Shea, and you've been taking liberties with my daughter. Now what part of this plan do you expect I think is working?"

"What if I just leave town? Never come back? You and Louisa will never see me again, I swear it! No harm done, and I'll be gone for good."

"It's a bit late for no harm done, O'Connor." Lundgren drew his gun.

Neither man heard the depot door open behind them, nor did they hear Harlan Shea as he entered the doorway just behind Lundgren.

"Best lower that gun nice and slow," Shea said. "I don't relish the idea of shooting a fella in the back. Not even if he's about to commit murder."

The tensed muscles in Lundgren's neck and shoulders relaxed a bit.

"Put it on the desk there real easy. Now take a step over there toward the window and let's see if we can talk this out like reasonable men."

"Shea, you oughta learned by now to mind your own business."

"Anywhere I come across killers and rustlers, I make it my business."

"You seem to forget not all that long ago Haxton would have fit the bill of killer and rustler."

"I make a habit of not judging men by who they were before."

"You don't owe him anything, Shea. He fired you, humiliated you in front of the town. You rode off with your tail between your legs, the finest foreman around. Damned if I didn't hope you'd wander into Texas some day so as I could hire you for my outfit."

O'Connor's wandering eyes caught Shea's attention. Lundgren's Manhattan revolver lay just beyond his reach. "Don't think about going for that gun, boy," Shea warned. "I doubt you could lift it, let alone use it."

"It's not too late, Shea," Lundgren grunted. "After I finish my business here, ride with me down to Texas. I'll make you foreman. There won't be no rustlin', no more shenanigans. I've pulled my last stunt here. I've learned my lesson, seein' what it's done to my Louisa. I'm an honest man from this day forth."

Trouble at Timber Ridge

"You've said that before, I'm guessing," Shea said sardonically.

"It's a fine ranch, Shea. A few bad apples in the outfit from the old days, but you'd have no problem handling them. Hell, they'd run at the sight of you. There's a future down there in Texas, Shea, and it's ours for the taking."

Shea holstered his gun, thoughtfully. "I'll tell you what, Lundgren," Shea said. "Why don't you leave me to deliver junior here to the authorities, and then I'll come down to Texas and hear your offer? I imagine I can convince O'Connor here to implicate himself in his confession and not incriminate you."

"I can't do that, Shea."

"Bet I could even talk Haxton into not pressing charges, so long as O'Connor here was safely behind bars and unable to make further mischief."

"I said I can't do it, Shea."

"Because of Louisa?"

"Because of Louisa."

"I don't reckon she'd wait all that long for this little weasel to serve his time before she started receiving other callers, do you?"

O'Connor's green eyes narrowed, and his lips firmed into a white line.

"Why, with your permission, Lundgren, maybe I could come by the ranch and pay her my respects."

"It's not that simple, Shea," Lundgren said. "It might have been once. I'd tell a man that would've been fine. But it can't be, not anymore."

"So you do know," Shea said.

"Know what?" O'Connor asked.

"She's grown up," Shea said. "Made her own decisions."

"No," Lundgren said. "I don't accept that."

"And the more you urged her to keep her distance..."

"Mind your words, Shea."

"You sowed these here seeds, Lundgren. I reckon you earned the right to reap."

Lundgren's eyes darkened, as though heavy winter storm clouds had rolled in behind them, while at the same time an air of unnatural calm swept over him. Shea knew he was no longer in the room with a rancher. The old gunfighter Lundgren was standing before him.

Lundgren pivoted quickly, and his hand darted for the revolver on the table. But when his hand reached the gun, it met O'Connor's. At the same time, O'Connor's other hand shot up and jabbed a thumb hard into the old gunfighter's eye. Lundgren batted wildly at the arm causing him pain.

As O'Connor struggled vainly for control of the revolver, he twisted himself around the gunfighter. Now his back and head blocked Lundgren's vitals.

In the cramped telegraph office, there was no position from which Shea could get off a safe shot. He stood, gun leveled, and waited.

As hard as O'Connor tried to control the gun, the certainty of his approaching end transformed O'Connor. The young man became a desperate, trapped animal. He stomped on Lundgren's forward foot, and kicked feebly at his shins. As quickly as a wolf leaps on a fleeing deer, he clamped his teeth on Lundgren's ear, tearing flesh and crunching cartilage.

Even as O'Connor bit off a piece of Lundgren's ear, the old outlaw managed to bring the barrel of the revolver to bear on Shea under O'Connor's scrawny arm. O'Connor jerked his head to the side, letting go of the ear, giving Shea a clear shot at Lundgren's forehead.

Lundgren instantly realized both his vulnerability and advantage. Two shots rang out so close together they sounded like one.

O'Connor's fingers let go of Lundgren's wrist as the old rancher fell, his head shattered. Along with the gunfighter's body, the revolver dropped to the floor. Slowly, O'Connor turned, empty hands raised in surrender. He tasted blood in his mouth. He spat out a significant chunk of Lundgren's ear and wiped a dribble of the other man's blood on the shoulder of his jacket, while he kept his hands above his head.

His eyes found Shea standing ready in the doorway, his face expressionless, the stance that of a born

Trouble at Timber Ridge

gunfighter. The gun was leveled from the hip. Shea's weathered Stetson tipped forward, masking his face in sinister shadow. The rim of the Stetson, O'Connor noticed, had a new hole through it, just a few inches above his left ear. And for the second time in as many minutes, O'Connor found himself faced with an insurmountable enemy and certain doom.

"Now, O'Connor, what do I do with you?" he asked, seeming unconcerned by his brush with death.

O'Connor's sickly complexion was deathly pale against his apple-red hair. His weak knees were failing him. He dropped his hands to support himself on the back of his chair. "Wait – please – don't shoot! I never intended to wrong nobody. Louisa, she blinded me – I'm mad for her, and I hate myself for it."

"Tell me how you two pulled this off," Shea prompted, keeping his Schofield leveled at O'Connor's mid-region.

"I came out here last year, from St. Louis. My father, he helped found the Brotherhood of Telegraphers. Haxton wrote them a letter asking for a man to run the new telegraph office. A few weeks after I settled in, Louisa arrived. She got a job working tables in O'Malley's under the name of Campbell. Said she was from Dodge City and was looking for clean, honest work. She sure made every man in this town go whistlin', even the old and married ones. When she first asked to receive me over at the hotel, I thought she was joking. I mean, she could have had any man in Timber Ridge, and she asked me. Just look at me!"

Shea felt sorry for O'Connor. Slight as a waif and pale, the young man had less meat on him than a starved burro, and a lanky, awkward frame suggested he was not likely to grow into much more of a man. The ridiculous red curls appeared untamable, and patchy stubble on his chin and cheeks meant trying to compensate for the softness of his freckled face with whiskers was not an option.

"But you went," Shea said.

"I went, and she came on strong. From then on, I was hogtied. I was crazy, I'd have done anything. I'd have killed a man for her."

Shea chuckled.

"Well, I'd have tried to anyway," O'Connor said, remembering. A dark cloud shadowed his expression for a moment, then was gone.

"How did she talk you into it?"

"On a Sunday, shortly after I started calling on her, she asked if I'd walk her home from church. We were conversing right well, and continued on past the hotel. As we were passing here, she asked if I'd show her where I worked. I was plumb excited, showed her the camelback Tillotson key over there and told her how it worked. She sort of batted her eyes and oohed and aahed over everything I said. Don't think she understood a word of it.

"When I showed her the ledger, she asked if all the telegrams got logged in there. I told her they did, if I didn't copy the codes down as they came through the wire, I'd lose track. Then she asked what was to stop somebody from reading other people's private messages, and I said only me. I felt real important just then, too. She said I had men's destinies running through my fingers on ticker tape.

"Then she told me who she was, and a little bit of the story behind the bad blood between Haxton and Lundgren. She convinced me she needed my help putting things right, and how I wouldn't be harming anyone really. It wasn't like Haxton was going to be rustled out of cattle or anything. Her father just wanted a chance to earn back some of what Haxton stole from him years back. Least, that's where it started. It went a bit further, later.

"We hatched a plan. At first, we thought of using ciphers, like the Union soldiers used to, but we settled on my simply relaying any business-related messages to or from Haxton down to Lundgren. That way, if I ever got caught, I could claim it was an innocent mistake.

"By the time I had my wits about me, I was in the mix thick. I knowed the scheme couldn't hold up much longer

Trouble at Timber Ridge

or I'd be found out for sure. I couldn't come forward, Haxton's outfit would have done me in. I'm no fighter, I'm a coward, and I was scared – scared to death.

"I tried to get Louisa to elope with me, but she refused. I'm not likely to land another good position after all this gets out, and I haven't saved a cent. I've spent everything I made trying to impress her. We'd be in for lean times for a while, and she knows that."

"That's why you two were quarreling," Shea said, knowing there had been more to their conversation than the boy would admit to, even now.

"I knew the whole thing would blow up eventually, but never even in my nightmares did I figure it would be Lundgren comin' for me. Must have wanted to keep me from talking."

"Among other things, I reckon," Shea answered.

"Give me a chance, will you? To put things right? I'll do anything you say."

"Damn right you will," Shea said, putting his gun away. "You'll start by marrying Louisa."

"What?" The boy was stunned. "You're – you're not going to shoot me?"

"I figure Colorado's got all the bastards she needs."

O'Connor stared at him blankly.

"Didn't you know? Louisa's in the family way."

O'Connor's face flashed from white to scarlet.

"Well, what was it you thought made Lundgren come and blow the cover off this little scheme of his?"

The boy stared down at the still-warm body of his would-be father-in-law on the floor.

"With that marriage," the cowboy continued, "you'll be comin' into a bit of money. I figure eighty, ninety thousand dollars worth of ranch and cattle."

"Ninety thousand..." O'Connor muttered.

Shea saw the boy's legs wouldn't hold up under him much longer and helped him into his chair.

"Plenty to set up nice for Louisa and Junior," Shea said. "You'll be in a position to care for her. Buy her nice things. Give her a future, better than any man I know. Even after you pay off your debt."

"Debt?" O'Connor said, snapping out of his daze. "But I don't have any d—" He cut himself short as he realized what Shea meant.

"That's right. As soon as the preacher's done with you, you'll march over to the bank and write out a hefty promissory note to Haxton for what your lovemaking cost him. Then, you happy little lovebirds can hop on the next train back to White Pines for the honeymoon.

"You'll get the money I figure you owe Haxton by the end of two months. Or there's gonna be one more red-headed kid in Texas without a father."

O'Connor sighed heavily. "I never figured things would turn out like this when I left St. Louis."

"No, I don't suppose you did. You came out here thinking you knowed more about the modern world than a rabbit does about running. And it took under a year to make you into an old-fashioned crook with an illegitimate child in the belly of a dead outlaw's daughter. But you're getting off easy at that. After all, you're getting set up nice with a beautiful wife and a nice little ranch down in Texas."

"What do I know about running a ranch?" O'Connor asked, staring down at his feet.

"Oh, not much, I imagine. But Louisa'll fire Lundgren's outfit and you can hire yourself a young, ambitious foreman to run the place for you. Besides, that little woman of yours knows ranches, though I wouldn't recommend letting her hold the ropes for you, at least not publicly."

"But what if she won't marry me?"

"What other choice does she have? Her pa's dead at your feet, O'Connor, and there'll be a baby to care for."

O'Connor's face darkened again, and hell fire sparked behind those green eyes. "What if she loves someone else?" he asked, through gritted teeth.

"What the hell's love got to do with it, O'Connor? She's in a tight spot, and you're responsible for putting her there. So buck up and do the right thing, or..." Shea gestured toward his pistol, "...take your chances with me."

Trouble at Timber Ridge

O'Connor stared at him for a long while with hate in his eyes. *Well, you can't choose a man's fate for him,* Shea thought. *Each has to choose his own trails.* "Life's like a dirty dream, son. It's confusing, messy, and it's over all too quick. Best not to over-think a good thing, just enjoy it, while it lasts."

The young man cast a last, longing look at the little desk with its carefully smoothed ticker tapes, fancy brass key, and leather bound ledger. He shook his head to clear it, tossed the door key on the desk, and then shuffled out and down the dusty street.

The small, silent crowd gathered outside, drawn to the sound of gunfire like crows to carrion, parted as he passed through.

Doc Emerson peered hesitantly through the door before stepping in. "Is that man dead?" He asked. A little runny egg yolk clung stubbornly to his whiskers.

"Yup," Shea responded.

"All right," Emerson said. "Guess you don't need me then, I'll go finish my breakfast. Sheriff went over to Waldschmidt's just a little while ago, and I imagine he'll be tied up there for a spell."

"Well, Lundgren's not going any place," Shea said. He grabbed the door key off the desk, locked the body in the office, and drew the diminutive curtains over the window, much to the chagrin of a few curious boys on tiptoes.

Chapter 17

After Louisa had left the house, Dan went straight away to talk to Sheriff Reddington. When he returned, he took his time walking the mare into the corral and slid the bar latch closed. His face had aged beyond his years in wind and weather. But he still had the confident stride and high head of a young stallion, giving an agelessness to his overall appearance.

As soon as he walked into the house and saw his wife paging through the yellow, moldy family bible, he knew something was troubling her. Mary talked silently with her Savior for some time. She pleaded, as she had a hundred times before that her womb might be opened, that she might raise sons with Dan. And if not, she prayed that healthy, young Louisa might decide to give up her baby.

Mary's heart was adrift in sea of guilt and excitement. She realized her kindness toward Louisa had been rooted in selfish motives. And she realized she had not the contrition to do anything to change it.

In her mind, she could only hope and pray that her just recompense would not be meted out upon her and the man she loved...

_*_ _*_ _*_

"Hello, Louisa," Shea said, holding his hat in his hands.

"Was that gunfire I heard?" she asked, without turning from the fireplace in the hotel parlor.

"I'm afraid so," he answered.

She tensed visibly. "I hoped I imagined it. Who..." she started, choking back a sob.

"O'Connor is fine," Shea said simply. "I'm sorry, Louisa. I only did what I had to."

Trouble at Timber Ridge

She spun around, fists at her side, fire in her eyes. "You monster! Murderer! Harlan Shea, how could you?"

Shea never flinched. He stood across the parlor, turning his hat in his hands absently, watching her with a gaze both intense and expressionless. As quickly as it flamed, the fire in her eyes died down and her hands relaxed.

"Did he try to hurt Alvis?"

"Tried to shoot him, but O'Connor fought back."

"Alvis is not much for the likes of Pa, I guess."

"He has a will to live at least," Shea said, diplomatically.

"And you, are you hurt?"

"No, ma'am, I'm fine."

"I feel weak, I think I need to sit down," she said.

He moved to assist her into a chair.

"Stop! Don't touch me! I ... I need to think."

He stepped back again as she slumped onto a couch.

"Harlan Shea, you saved my fiancé from my Pa and killed him in the process. I don't know whether to thank you or hate you. Pa had it coming, I know. I begged Pa not to go over there. I thought if I talked with him, maybe..." She put her hands to her face and cried.

"Oswald must have told Pa," she continued after he took a seat beside her on the couch. "He came here right when he got to town. He called me – he called me terrible things...and he hit me." She wept for several long moments. "I've always known he'd be killed someday. I've dreaded the day, and yet ... Oh, it's too horrible, I can't say it, what I feel. It's more like ... more like relief than sorrow."

"It was a fair fight, he got a shot off at me too. He died like a man," Shea said, thinking of how different her dead, outlaw father was from the man she would marry. *But O'Connor may grow into a man yet,* Shea thought.

"Pa admired you, Harlan, you know that, don't you? He often talked of your return, longed for it as much as he feared it. He used to say, if Shea ever shows up at White Pines, I'll either hire him or kill him. You put the fear of God into him when he and the boys went up against Haxton. I was just a girl then, fourteen, but I remember, he came back a changed man. Not quite fearless anymore. He'd seemed bigger than life to me before, but was mortal after that. Haunted. You broke something inside him in that fight, Harlan, and to fix it he knew he needed you either at his side or under his feet."

She rose and returned to her vigil at the empty fireplace. "Would he have killed Alvis, had you not showed up?"

"An unarmed boy against a gunfighter don't stand much of a chance," Shea said, quickly regretting his words.

"Unarmed! Oh, Pa! All this jealousy, all this anger – it brought out the worst in you in the end. And to think of the hand I played in all this. Harlan, I'm – I'm more complicit in his death than you are."

"Louisa," Shea started, as she turned to face him.

She fell against him, her tears penetrating the dam of her fingers and moistening his vest. He held tightly to her lithe body, glowing with the coming of motherhood, against his broad chest. Long, brown hairs caught against the stubble of his chin as she tucked the crown of her head beneath it.

"What a mess, Harlan," Louisa said, stifling a sob. "How low I've sunk! If I ever thought I loved Alvis, it was only because I wanted to think I was doing right. When I let him in my ... in my bed, I didn't ... love him then, Harlan. I feared him running, leaving me caught between Pa's wrath and the law, and alone. So alone."

After a moment, she pulled away from his embrace. "Louisa," he started a second time, but she pressed moist, warm fingertips against his lips.

"Don't, Harlan. It might have been, but my sins have sealed my fate now. I should never have let my loyalty to Pa cloud my sense of right and wrong. Now I see what a menace his bitterness was. What corruption hate causes! What ruin!"

"You have your whole life ahead of you, Louisa. We all have dark demons in our pasts. But the sun still rises every morning."

Trouble at Timber Ridge

She looked at him with watery blue eyes. "You would still have me after all this?"

"There's no man in Colorado who could resist falling in love with you, Louisa. Even now."

She smiled faintly. "Harlan Shea, there's more man in you than in all the west combined." She reached up and kissed him on the cheek, pulling away quickly.

Shea grabbed her arms fiercely and pulled her back to him.

"Harlan, you're hurting me—"

Her protest was smothered with kisses. Stern hands on her arms released, one searching around her narrow waist, the other exploring the silkiness of her brown hair. For a brief moment, all was forgotten, lost in the fog of passion. Then, he released her.

"Goodbye, Louisa," Shea said with a bow, and replaced his Stetson upon his head.

"Harlan, wait!" she said, but he was already out the door.

She ran to the window and stared after him. Her heart was a torrent of emotions as she watched the man who had been the instrument of her father's destruction. Guiltily, she knew she'd played her part in his demise as well. Gust Lundgren had made it plain that a final battle between he and Haxton was coming, and only one man could be left standing. The fates selected an odd collection of people to play a part in his final stand: a crooked telegraph officer, a disgraced cowpuncher, even his own daughter. The entire tragedy had the air of inevitability to it. As she stood there, an overwhelming sense of loss seized her, and her knees trembled.

But loss of who or what? She had loved her father, even as she hated him. And she had long since resigned herself to his violent end, much as he had himself. Of Alvis? Certainly, fear had changed him. He had come to Timber Ridge young, cosmopolitan, and sophisticated. He had not been much to look at, but he had excited her with his talk of taking her back east to a life of luxury, decadent parties, and respectable society. Young women were drawn to urban culture like moths to a flame.

Fear had degraded O'Connor. Like a scared, wild animal, he seemed to think only of self-preservation. And while she may well have agreed to elope with the proud, city boy who had come to Timber Ridge months before, the weak, frightened O'Connor who jumped at shadows was someone she could never love or even respect. Then, what loss troubled her so deeply, down to her soul?

As she stood at the window, watching Shea enter the saloon across the road, unseen eyes were watching her from just outside the room. They were green eyes that saw clearly what troubled her, more clearly than she could see herself. They glared beneath a mop of untamable red curls. Quietly, Alvis O'Connor snuck back down the hall of the hotel just as Shea got up to leave, and through the back door into the alley. He took a modest gold band from his pocket, and inspected it briefly. He had sent for his mother's wedding ring several weeks earlier, before Lundgren's plan had begun to unravel. His father had happily posted it, along with a letter stating his hopes to meet the fine young western girl who had so captured his son's attentions. A little western blood might reinvigorate the O'Connor line, his father had said, subtly suggesting his disappointment in his only son, as he often did.

O'Connor pocketed the ring, and sat down on the bare ground to think. He leaned up against the back of the hotel, and thought long and hard about Louisa Lundgren, and how to exact his revenge.

Chapter 18

Shea went directly from the hotel to O'Malley's tavern, swung open the batwings, and found an empty chair next to Haxton and Perloe, who were using bits of bread to swab up some bean juice.

"Thought I heard a gunshot down by the depot," Haxton said, chewing.

"You heard two."

"You're still here, so who's dead?"

"Lundgren."

"Oh. Didn't know he was in town. Might have shot him myself, had I known."

"Rode in this morning, early, to run the O'Connor kid out of town, I think."

"So, he knew our telegraph agent?"

"Louisa's his daughter."

The rancher stared up at him. "His daughter?"

"He sent her up here to entice O'Connor into intercepting your and Fairbault's messages and redirect them when it suited him. That's why he had the second set of books."

Perloe piped up over glasses barely perched upon the tip of his knows. "It's a shame you killed him, Mr. Shea, before he confessed. Now, I've nothing but your good word as evidence when I report back to Fairbault."

"I had to kill him, Perloe. When I got there, he was seeing red. I think he would have killed the boy had I not shown up."

Haxton swallowed a slug of coffee, and said, "The kid probably deserved it, but why did Lundgren turn so suddenly on his co-conspirator?"

"Louisa's pregnant." A hushed understanding enveloped the table. "I gave the boy a talkin' to. He and

Louisa are going back to Texas to White Pines, but he'll send you some money to make up for the losses he caused inside of two months."

"Hmm," Haxton sat quiet and thoughtful for a moment. "So, Lundgren finally got his. But I don't know which was the greater justice, being shot or getting that skinny redheaded city boy for a son-in-law." Haxton chuckled, washed down the last bit of bread with a swallow of coffee, then sat back in his chair with his hands on his belly. After a moment, he said, "The boy can keep his money, if it means this feud is ended."

"I reckon he'd take you up on that. I recommended he fire that outfit what's caused all the trouble, and hire fresh. But he'll lose a fair bit of green, I'd wager, until he figures out how a ranch is run."

"That's probably true."

Perloe chimed in. "Well, if you aren't the hero of the day, Mr. Shea. And after saving the city boy's life, and knowing how he can't know a bloody thing concerning a ranching operation, am I to presume that for further inquiries regarding the Lonsdale incident, I'm to contact you at White Pines?"

"I'm not sure I recall agreeing to any such inquiries," Shea replied.

"Well, I took the liberty of sending a telegram to my Lonsdale friends just yesterday, informing them of your whereabouts, and encouraging us all to have a sit down to talk—"

"Mr. Perloe, it's not sitting and talking they'll be wanting to do with me. Actually, I think I'll head for the hills for a while. You see, when those Lonsdale boys catch up to me, there's gonna be a lot of blood spilt, and I'm in no rush to spill it. And Mr. Perloe, your buddies over in Lonsdale, I wouldn't turn my back on them, if I was you."

"To tell you the truth, Mr. Shea, my colleagues are as suspicious of the men on your tail as they are of you. Maybe more so. I half hoped that your testimony might help bring several Lonsdale ranchers to justice."

"You want Harlan here to condemn the party that's out to lynch him?" Haxton asked. "At the risk of his own

Trouble at Timber Ridge

neck? And who knows how many other lives wasted in the process. Harlan, I think I'd have no part in that if I was you. Head for the hills, I say. Before those Lonsdale folks come to town. Lie low for a while, and when the dust settles..." Haxton smiled, "...maybe come see me about a job."

Together, the three got up from the table and walked through the batwings, squinting in the brilliant sunlight. Haxton limped stiffly, the old wound aggravated by prolonged sitting. Shea reflected that the man who had ended Haxton's riding days could do no further harm, as he helped the rancher up into his buckboard.

Haxton picked up the reins and stared through the dust into the distance. "Much as I'd like you to stay on and work for me again, I can't imagine there's much left to hold you here," Haxton said.

"I sure do appreciate the offer, boss," Shea said.

"You were the best damn foreman I ever had, Shea, despite the drinkin' and the temper."

"Someday, I figure, I'll be yearnin' again for the clang of the supper bell and the comfort of a bunk to call my own. But not yet, not just yet."

"Well, when that day comes, you'll know where to find me," Haxton said. He snapped the reins on the horse's rump and was off.

Shea stood there thinking as he watched Haxton and Perloe ride down the road toward the ranch.

Then Shea saw O'Connor duck around from behind the hotel, and hurry toward the church. "Looks like O'Connor made his choice," Shea said. "For now, at least." With that, he mounted his mare, slapped her flank and rode out of Timber Ridge toward the mountains.

_-*- -*- -*-_

Less than a quarter mile down the road, Dan and Mary Waldschmidt were sitting at coffee with Sheriff Reddington when they were interrupted by a knock on the door. Dan got up to answer it. He was surprised to find Louisa standing on his porch, bag in hand. She was watching over her shoulder nervously. Waldschmidt stepped onto the porch and looked around, but not seeing anything, took the bag from her and invited her in.

"Pa's dead," she told them. "He came to town to kill Alvis, and Harlan shot him."

"Shot him, did he?" Reddington asked.

"Louisa, I'm sorry," Waldschmidt said.

"Pa had it coming for a long time."

"Have you told Mr. O'Connor about the baby?" Mary asked.

"I can't. I-I don't love Alvis. And I'd sooner sell White Pines than let him bungle it. Is it too late to change my mind, Mr. Waldschmidt?" she asked.

"No, miss, you're still welcome here."

"So, Shea shot your Pa and saved the father of your baby, is that it?" Reddington asked.

"Oh, can't it wait, Mr. Reddington?" Mary asked. "The poor dear has been through so much today."

"I guess I'm taking you and Mr. Waldschmidt up on your offer, then," Louisa said. "Heaven knows I'll need some help, until the baby comes. After that, I-I don't know what I'll do."

"We can worry about that later," Dan said.

"We have plenty of room," Mary continued. "And there's work on the ranch afterward, too; you can help me in the house and the laundry..."

"She grew up on a ranch," Waldschmidt said, chuckling. "She's as likely to be breaking horses as doing laundry."

"You two have been too kind to me," Louisa said.

"Oh, it's only Christian, child," Mary said. "Now come here and let me show you to your bed." The two women set down their coffee and stepped through the cramped kitchen into the other room.

"Looks like she's been through it," Waldschmidt said.

"Reckon I oughta head back into town," Reddington said, patting his belly. "I'll look into this business of yours promptly, Waldschmidt, as soon as I sort out this business of Shea shooting Gust Lundgren. Thank Mary for the coffee," he added, stretching and heading for the door.

Trouble at Timber Ridge

In the cabin, Mary was arranging Louisa's things in an old, creaky dresser. "It's not much, but it should do," she said. "Darling, are you all right? You've been staring out that window since you walked in this room."

"Just thinking, Mary."

"You loved him, didn't you?"

"Yes, I guess I did."

"Well, any boy who cheats and steals wouldn't make much of a husband or a father anyway."

"Cheats and steals?" she asked, genuine confusion in her voice. "Oh – oh, I'm sorry, I was thinking of someone else."

Mary looked at her quietly for a moment, perplexity knotting her brow. Then she left the girl to her thoughts.

Having just turned back to the cabin from having seen Reddington off, Waldschmidt also noticed the girl standing at the bedroom window staring fixedly toward the distance. Following her gaze, Waldschmidt saw a trail of dust kicked up by a rider, galloping up the road toward the mountains. Although he couldn't make out the rider at such great distance, Waldschmidt had his suspicions.

Almost unnoticed, Mary joined her husband on the porch. "Dan, I think there's even more to Louisa's troubles than she's let on."

"Yes, Mary, I think you're right. A few nights ago, I saw Louisa and some fellah talkin' up in the hotel parlor. I couldn't tell definite who it was, but he was a lot bigger than O'Connor and roughly dressed."

"Who was it?" Mary asked.

"I do believe it was Harlan Shea."

"Shea?" Mary asked with incredulity. "Oh, I had hoped it was someone more seemly."

"Mary, I rode under Shea as foreman for years before Lundgren shot Haxton. He was rough, a fighter and a drinker in those days, and I'll admit I don't know all that much about him or his past. But I do know this. He's strong and he's loyal. I wasn't in the least bit surprised when Haxton called him in for help with his recent troubles. Were I Haxton, I would have done the same."

"But there's no name in these parts more feared than Harlan Shea," Mary said. "Oh, I do hope she hasn't fallen in love with that man."

"You know, Mary, even in his devilish days, Shea was a good man through and through. A trustworthy man. A friend. If he's cast aside the demon of drink, well, I can't imagine a man more capable to protect and provide for her."

"Is Shea still in town?"

"No, I think he's just leaving," Waldschmidt said, nodding toward the trail of dust in the distance.

"Are you going after him?" Mary asked.

"I suppose I am." He stepped off the porch and a moment later grabbed his saddle off the corral fence.

_*_ _*_ _*_

When O'Connor left the hotel, he walked toward the church, but had no intention of seeking out the minister. Holy matrimony was, in fact, the furthest thing from his mind. O'Connor passed the church, crossed the street, and bounded up the steps of Morgan's boarding house, where he had resided since arriving in Timber Ridge. Morgan was a good landlord, in the sense that he kept out the way and didn't ask many questions. While the hotel was the place to stay when visiting Timber Ridge on business, Morgan's was preferred by those whose business was conducted in whispered tones. At the moment, it offered O'Connor a private room where he could hide out until he figured his next move.

Chapter 19

Harlan Shea was not the only one who saw O'Connor heading out from the hotel. From the shadows of the awning over the general store's porch, Oswald was watching and thinking. Lundgren was dead, he knew. He hadn't seen the body, but when he saw only O'Connor and Shea leaving the depot, there was no other conclusion to draw. How Shea had escaped from Henry and the cabin, he had no idea, but his fear of Shea had once again been validated.

What this meant for him was unclear. Lundgren's gang, which had been operating out of White Pines for years, would inevitably catch wind of their boss' demise. Oswald had been Lundgren's faithful second-in-command, and if he got back to White Pines quickly enough, both the ranch and the gang could be his. However, he had no intention of returning to White Pines without Louisa. Her father was dead – what would stop him from having her too? Besides, she would be the heiress of White Pines, which would offer the cover of legitimacy to his operation, should the law try to interfere.

But what was he to do about young Alvis O'Connor? It seemed likely that once her father was buried, O'Connor would marry Louisa, as unlikely a match as the beauty and the gangly red weasel seemed. But choices would be slim for the pregnant girl, and slimmer still for the unemployed greenhorn. Oswald had been at the ranch since Louisa was a child. He remembered the playful, innocent way the young girl had flirted with her father's men. She would climb the fence rails to watch the riders come in to corral. She teased them for their filth and begged them to mind their manners.

And as Oswald worked his tail to the bone toward fulfilling his ambition to be made foreman, Louisa grew into a beautiful woman. The schoolgirl coquettishness evolved into a young woman's deviousness. All those years of playful childhood practice with the hearts of men matured into a powerful skill.

Over more recent years, Louisa had shown him a woman's disdain toward a man whose looks lingered too long and wandered too far from her eyes. Any naive, playful trust in him she had as a child was gone, and Oswald had every reason to believe his position at White Pines was in jeopardy. What years of being a sycophant and doing dirty jobs had secured could be forever undone by a single word from Louisa. So, his feelings for her turned both lusty and resentful.

If Louisa married Alvis O'Connor, well, Oswald found the idea of working for O'Connor detestable in the extreme. But, even worse was the idea of Louisa and O'Connor sharing a bed. On the other hand, wouldn't Louisa be more likely to return to White Pines with O'Connor in tow than with Oswald alone? He was the father of her baby, after all. He would make sure, however, that the marriage would be short lived. Once O'Connor was out of the picture and Louisa was mistress of the ranch, Oswald would have it all: the ranch, the gang, and the girl.

Careful to stay clear of Shea's view, Oswald slunk around to the back door of Morgan's boarding house.

-*- -*- -*-

A well-needed rain had started to fall, dampening the soil and making Waldschmidt's job of following Shea into the unknown wilderness of the mountains somewhat easier. The heavy step of Delilah with her giant rider left clear prints along the trail into the lower swells. The rarely used trail was awash in webs along which small spiders scurried. The pines grew thick, their lower branches interlaced, giving them the look of skeletons guarding the trail. Among the pines were twisted, bare oaks whose branches reminded Dan of the arms of drowning men. The woods were unearthly quiet. As he climbed the mountainside, the pines and occasional oaks gave way to hunched boulders flaked with gray lichen. Small critters scurried among the rocks.

The shadows grew longer, and the trail began to disappear before his eyes. The stony earth yielded little spore of the leading rider; the trail became diffuse and uncertain. His horse stumbled some on the loosening stone.

Waldschmidt dismounted. This portion of the trail was treacherous, and he had no desire to risk his horse. Only a daredevil rider would risk a horse up a stretch of climb like this.

A little farther up, the ground leveled somewhat. Waldschmidt saw the first sight that suggested men had ever walked this way before. It was an earthen mound, just longer than a man stretched out. Obviously a grave, although there was no marker of any type, not even a pile of stones.

Somewhere, a wolf howled.

_*_ _*_ _*_

Oswald nudged the door open, and found O'Connor sitting disconsolate on the corner of the bunk. "He's dead, Oswald," O'Connor said. "It's over."

"I imagine you're right fine getting out anyway," Oswald said. "And now you and Louisa, well, I suppose you'll be getting hitched."

O'Connor couldn't bring himself to tell Oswald about Louisa kissing Shea.

"I figure you and she will be heading back for White Pines," Oswald said. "I wanted to offer my assistance. When the gang finds out the boss is dead, they'll take over the ranch. I thought I could help you secure it before it falls into other hands."

O'Connor looked at him skeptically. "And why would you want to help me?"

"There's going to be a new boss. I plan to be him. When Louisa inherits the ranch, and if I stay on as foreman, it'll all be quite legitimate. The gang can keep on using White Pines as our base of operations. As for you, well, you'd own a big, rich ranch in Texas. In the eyes of the law, at least."

O'Connor was silent while he thought. "What if Louisa doesn't want to go back to White Pines?" he asked.

"Not go back to the ranch that's rightfully hers? That don't seem likely. I'll go and talk to her. I'll find her and explain the situation, and how I'll help set you two up in the ranch and get the gang under control."

"And if she doesn't want to come?"

"Don't be stupid, O'Connor. What choice does she have? You think she'll give up the ranch to raise a baby in Timber Ridge? Anyway, I'm not leaving without her. Are you?"

-*- -*- -*-

The trail took Waldschmidt around a stony cliff face and into a pass unlike anything he had ever seen. Two peaks towered above him, rising from massive boulders, capped in steep tapers that rose like weary, ancient sentinels guarding the pass. Mounds of snow covered the rocky slopes, looking ready to slide to the ground. Waldschmidt slowed his horse to a snail's pace for fear that even the echoes of horseshoes from the rocky trail might precipitate an avalanche and close the pass.

At its far end, the silent pass sloped downward into a dark, low wood, seemingly too dense for the altitude, but then Dan could not tell how high he'd climbed or descended as the oppressive cliffs on either side disoriented him. He caught glances of game flickering among the shadows. As he descended, he passed two more unmarked graves. The cliffs narrowed, engulfing what must have been a few dozen acres in a shallow bowl blocked off on all sides but for the pass. Jagged cliffs encompassed the hidden valley like the walls of an ancient castle, broken only at the pass, the one way in or out of the wooded oasis.

The wood was cool, but provided welcome shelter from the wind which howled through the pass. It was more accessible than his first glance let on, though he had dismounted and led his horse on foot. He smelled pine smoke somewhere near. A couple yards into the wood, he

Trouble at Timber Ridge

found a fourth earthen mound. When the trees thickened, Waldschmidt tied his horse to a hearty birch and continued alone.

"Fellow could settle in here indefinitely," he muttered. There were trees aplenty for firewood and, judging by the tracks, abundant game. Waldschmidt stepped through a thin veil of pine and thorns. The wood was dark, with thick trunks of trees standing like columns in a vast cathedral. The sky could barely be seen through the leafy boughs. He stepped cautiously and studied the brush, leaves, and trees until he realized he was standing in a path of sorts, either an old Indian trail or a game trail. He followed it warily, and eventually the brush thickened again and he had to crouch under a bough here, and step over a fallen log there.

In a small clearing, a long-abandoned campsite had been overgrown with brush. There were crates of tins scattered about. Thorn bushes encompassed crudely assembled tent frames, long vacated. There were stacks of firewood, rotted and nearly dirt at the base. The campsite had been abandoned hastily, long ago, it seemed to him.

"You looking for someone?" a man's voice said behind him. Waldschmidt spun and saw the giant form of Harlan Shea emerge from the trees and brush as though out of fog.

"Thank God it's you, Shea, I nearly died of fright."

"It's an eerie side of the mountain, ain't it?"

"Is this where you've been holed up all these years?"

"These past few years, and before."

"What is this place?"

"I grew up here. Pa was a trapper, and when I was about nine we were camping near here. We were cleaning up a spring for drinking water when we found gold. Pa built a cabin over yonder and we spent a season gatherin' what we could, but Pa soon decided it wasn't much of a strike. He left me to watch the cabin while he went down from the mountains to see about selling the claim.

"Four men bought in right quick. This here was their camp. But after a couple weeks, they figured the deposit wasn't all that rich, and started demanding that Pa return their money. The situation got tense. Then, the winter storms came on early, and unusually fierce. The men panicked when they realized they'd be walking their mounts miles out of the mountains over ice and snow. They never did make it down."

"So, those were the graves I saw on the way here?"

"Yeah."

"The cold got them?"

"No. It was a mistake to go after Pa."

They emerged in a clearing where an old, moss-covered cabin stood with inviting sweet pine smoke flowing from the chimney, and warm firelight seeping through the cracks in the boarded windows.

"Is this your hideout?" Waldschmidt asked.

"This is my home, my father's home. He's buried over there by the tree where they hung him." Shea pointed to a grave where a pile of stones formed a marker a few yards from the cabin.

"Wait, we're miles from anywhere. If they hung him, then who killed—" Waldschmidt stopped, as the truth hit him.

There was a shriek in the trees above, and the great falcon swooped down and perched on Shea's shoulder. The thought of young Shea – not yet ten years old – hunting down four men through ice and snow and rockslides, picking them off one by one like so many squirrels in the woods as they led their horses down the mountains. *What kind of boy would have the nerve to keep after four armed men until all were dead? Or, the stealth and the cunning to finish the job?* He imagined young Shea, creeping along in the bitter cold and icy screaming wind, hiding behind trees, biding his time until he could draw a bead on one of them with his Pa's rifle, and then dodging the inevitable return fire.

He thought of those graves, scattered over a couple miles through and beyond the pass. Young Shea had been in no hurry to finish the job. Instead of picking them off in a single ambush, he took them out one-by-one. His father's killers must have been driven half-mad, never knowing when the next shot would be fired, or from where, or who among them would fall. The image was disturbing.

"Come in," Shea said.

The cabin was crudely but adequately furnished with two modest bunks, a large, inviting fireplace, and a sizable bench for scraping hides and tending firearms. The old trapper's accouterments were neatly hung on antlers on the walls and from the rafters. The smell of biscuits baking in the ashes at the foot of the fireplace filled the air. Dan sat by the fire and removed his wet clothes, and Shea gave him an old Indian blanket to warm himself.

"What brings you all this way, Dan?"

"After you left, Louisa came to our place."

"What did she want?"

"Well, she's left O'Connor. And Mary ... well, you know women with their instincts. Mary thinks she's some heartsick over you leaving."

The giant gunslinger towered over Dan, who sat cross-legged by the fire. Shadows leapt and pranced madly along the walls. Shea remained silent, deep in thought.

"Mary thought you ought to know," Waldschmidt continued. "I think she half hopes Louisa will give up the baby. Mary and me, well we've wanted a baby of our own for some time, but it don't seem to be in the Lord's plan. But she's taken a genuine liking for the girl, and with her pa dead..."

"With her pa dead," Shea interrupted, "she ought to have gone back to the baby's father for support."

"She won't marry him, Shea. She doesn't love him and she doesn't think he could provide for them anyway. Mary says she's not too keen on raising his child, at least not on her own."

"She'll have White Pines. Whether she stays or sells, that should be enough for her to live off of."

"When it reaches White Pines that Lundgren is dead, the gang will take over the ranch. It's been their base of operations for years now. Sure, there'll be some fighting among them until somebody takes over as the new boss. But it was only their fear of Lundgren that made it a safe place for Louisa to live. She'll need a good gunhand to take back her inheritance."

"Why are you telling me this?"

"Mary and me, well we thought you might want to know."

"Damn it, Waldschmidt, look at me! I'm no husband, no father. Look around you, is this the kind of place to raise a baby?"

"I know a good man – a man I owe everything – who was reared in this very place," Waldschmidt said.

"My line is cursed, and it wouldn't be fair to pass that along to the child who's not even a rightful heir to the name of Shea."

"Don't know much about curses myself, but I do know you're sweet on that Louisa, and she's taken a real likin' to you. I know the kind of man you are, the kind of friend you've been. What you did for me, back on the day, taking the blame for..."

"There's no need to bring that up."

"You gave everything up to protect me, and that's the kind of man it takes to be a husband and a father."

Shea was silent for a long time, and perched himself on the edge of the lower bunk. He rubbed the scruff growing on his chin and looked thoughtful. Then he said, "Sheas don't make very good fathers, you know."

"How do you mean?"

"We're wild, for one thing. My granddad left my Pa fatherless for his love of Indian fighting. My Pa ... well ... I was orphaned before I was ten."

"So after you ... you killed the men who got your father, you came back here? Raised yourself? Alone?"

Shea said nothing.

"It's awful lonesome, Shea. What are you clinging to, up here? There's a beautiful girl in town, who loves you. She needs you."

Shea and Waldschmidt watched the fire in silence for some time. There was no more talking that night, save for Shea's suggestion that he ride back with Dan. In the morning, Shea and Waldschmidt gathered the horses and made for Dan's place near Timber Ridge. They rode out of the woods, through the silent pass and down the mountain, in no particular hurry.

An hour later, they broke through from the woods and headed to the Waldschmidt ranch.

Mary met them, running down the trail, as fast as her short, unsteady legs could carry her. Her eyes were red and puffy, and there was blood on her blouse. "Dan!" she yelled. "Oh, Dan, hurry! They took her! O'Connor, and a man called Oswald. They took Louisa!"

Chapter 20

While Waldschmidt and Shea were riding silently through the ominous, snow-peaked mountain pass that morning, Oswald was knocking on the Waldschmidts' door.

"Dan's not home," Mary said through the partially opened door. "Come back later."

"It's not Dan I'm looking for," Oswald replied. "I need to speak to Louisa. I heard she might be here. It's urgent. I'm a friend of her father's."

"Whom shall I tell her is calling?"

"Tell her it's Oswald, and she must hurry."

Mary closed the door and went to the bedroom, where she gently shook Louisa. "I'm sorry to wake you, but there's a man at the door who says he's a friend of your father's."

"Who is he?" Louisa asked, a chill running up her spine although she couldn't say why.

"Says his name is Oswald."

"What does he want?" Louisa asked, sitting upright.

"Says he needs to talk to you."

"Tell him I'm indisposed."

"He says it's urgent."

Louisa padded on bare feet to the door, and opened it warily, allowing only her face to show in the crack. "What do you want?"

"Louisa," Oswald said. "Can't I come in?"

"I don't want to see you now. Can't it wait?"

"It's the gang, Louisa. They'll be taking White Pines when they find out about your Pa."

"Don't you think I know that?"

"I can help them see right, Louisa. I was your Pa's second, and they'll accept me as the new boss. I can help

Trouble at Timber Ridge

them see having you and your new husband in the ranch house will keep the law at bay. But we need to go soon, before the news..."

"I'm not going to have a new husband."

"But O'Connor ... the baby..." Oswald stammered.

"I'm staying here in Timber Ridge for now. What I decide to do after that is my affair." She began to close the door, but he held it firmly.

"Hold on there, Louisa," Oswald said. "I don't know what's gotten into you. O'Connor's getting horses and supplies ready for us right now. He's going to be waiting for us just outside of town. Grab your things, we're going."

"Is everything all right, Louisa?" Mary asked from behind her.

"Fine, Mary," Louisa said, pressing harder on the door. "Oswald was just leaving."

"Like hell!" he growled, and shouldered the door open, knocking both women to the floor. He grabbed Louisa by the wrist and yanked her up. She screamed as he lifted her with an arm around her slender waist, and hurried her to his horse.

"Oswald, you're hurting me!" she yelled. Her bare feet scraped against the ground as he dragged her from the porch.

"I gave you a chance to come along nicely, Louisa," Oswald said.

"Louisa!" Mary yelled, pulling herself off the floor and running into the yard after them.

As Louisa struggled against Oswald's firm hold, Mary grabbed his jacket and hung on. Oswald whirled and elbowed her in the face, breaking her nose. Mary fell in the dust, blood running down her upper lip.

Louisa was more difficult to control than Oswald had counted on. He threw the wildly struggling girl on her knees by the horse he'd tied to a fence rail a short distance from the porch. "I hoped we could sort this out like old friends, Louisa."

Louisa sat in the dirt and rubbed her scraped feet. "Rot in hell, Oswald. I'm not going with you."

"Then we'll do this the hard way," Oswald said. He pulled out a pistol and put it to Mary's temple. Mary squeezed her eyes tight, and a trickle of tears ran from the corners. "Either you come with me or she dies."

"Mary, I'm so sorry I brought you into this," Louisa said, climbing on Oswald's horse.

"That's a good girl now," Oswald said. He grabbed a lariat and bound her arms tight. Then, he mounted behind her and gagged her with a bandana. He took the reins in one hand, and put his pistol against Louisa's ribs. "No more trouble." He tipped his hat to Mary, who was crying silently on the ground, and rode off.

When Oswald got Louisa to town, he guided the horse around the backs of the stores and into the woods. The winding trail rose through the wooded bluff behind O'Malley's tavern and was so thin and rocky that the horse had to walk much of the way. Eventually, they came to an old, abandoned trapper's cabin. The roof was alive with moss under a wind-tossed carpet of leaves and pine needles. The windows were merely wood shutters. A stovepipe jutted up from one side but had rusted partly away. A thin trail of gray smoke rose from it. A horse stood, tied up beside the cabin.

Oswald helped Louisa down from the horse, and marched her into the cabin. As the door creaked open, Louisa noticed bloody handprints on the door jam. A few flies crept along the stains, suggesting they were quite fresh.

"There's my bride," O'Connor said, stepping from the shadows and removing Louisa's gag.

"Alvis? Is that what all this is about? If I won't marry you willingly, you'll make me consent at gunpoint?"

"If having my baby in your belly isn't enough cause for you to marry me, than perhaps Oswald's gun might do the trick."

"How exactly do you think this will work, Alvis? You force me to consent to marriage, and then we go back to White Pines and live happily ever after?"

"O'Connor, I'd like a word, outside," Oswald said.

Trouble at Timber Ridge

The two men stepped into the yard. "Seems I've no further use for you, O'Connor."

"But ... I thought you were going to help..."

"O'Connor, I've got Louisa, no thanks to you. And as I can't see any reason now to take you back to White Pines, our partnership ends here." He pulled out his pistol and aimed it at O'Connor's head.

"Wait, Oswald," he said. "I can make her see reason. Wouldn't it be easier if she came willingly? Give me a chance to put things right with her."

The idea of Louisa coming back willingly to White Pines was appealing. After all, transporting an uncooperative captive all those miles on horseback was more than Oswald had bargained for.

"You've minutes to prove it's worth it to me to let you live," Oswald said.

O'Connor hurried into the cabin. "I'm no fool, Louisa. You've fallen in love with Harlan Shea. I heard you at the hotel. I saw you kiss him."

"He forced himself upon me!" she barked, the violence in her response betraying her conflicted feelings about the incident.

"But he didn't have to, did he? No, I don't expect you will consent to marry me and come back with me to White Pines. Make no mistake, that option is still open to you. But the alternative, the one I imagine you'll take, is that Oswald kills me and takes you by force. I think you loved me once, Louisa. Perhaps I could make you love me again. Would it be so bad? Marrying me? I mean, compared to what Oswald might ... what Oswald would do to you?

"Shea left you, Louisa. Oswald watched him ride out of Timber Ridge. He's gone and you'll never see him again. I may not be as big as him or as handy with a gun, but I never left you, and I never will."

Louisa braced herself against the wall of the cabin and smoothed her skirts. "Alvis, when we met, you have to understand, you were different from any man I'd ever known. You were well-traveled, cultured, witty, smart. You were also gentle and refined, so unlike the men I grew up among. So unlike Oswald..." she said, not caring whether the foreman outside could hear. "I imagined us moving back east, raising kids in nice schools, going to dinner parties and balls. I would have done anything for such a life." She paused.

"This," she gestured at him, "isn't what I loved. You're every bit the thief, kidnapper, extortionist my father was, and all his men are. You'll never be my husband. You'll never be the father of my child. It takes a man to be those things."

He struck her hard across the cheek, nearly knocking her to the floor. But she was ready for the second blow, and her chin came up quickly afterward. She looked him right in the eyes, proud and straight. "Go on, Alvis, you cowardly little child. All I have to do is call in Oswald and tell him I won't marry you, and he'll kill you. Go on. Strike me again."

O'Connor lowered his voice to a whisper, "Louisa, we can run. We can run back east, away from Oswald, away from the gang. My father has a big house in St. Louis – it's yours! We can escape. Away from all these ruffians, from all these guns, I'll be the man you thought I was. I promise you."

"You fool. Even if I agreed, do you think Oswald would let us get away that easily?"

"It's a long way to Texas, and he has to sleep sometime."

Oswald burst through the door. "O'Connor, come out here," he said in a hushed voice.

O'Connor stared at him, hate smoldering in his eyes. He stormed out after Oswald. "What is it?"

"Look!" Oswald pointed to the sky. A lone falcon was circling high above the cabin.

"Tell me that's not Shea's bird. He's coming already, isn't he?" O'Connor said, a slight quiver in his voice. "Damn it, Oswald, how does he know about this place?"

"Where do you think Henry and me were supposed to hold him until Lundgren got to town?"

Trouble at Timber Ridge

O'Connor reddened. "He loves her, you know. If he comes for her, we could maybe use him. Make her choose. Either she comes to White Pines, or Shea dies."

"There's a thought," Oswald said, through gritted teeth. He stood thinking for a moment. "He won't dare act up if we've a gun on her. Come to think of it, the last time I was on the wrong end of Shea's barrels, he was trapped in a small cabin not much bigger than this one," he said.

O'Connor looked about the small clearing. The horses were tied to fallen timbers beside the cabin. A muddied spring was a few paces from the cabin door, and looked like it would take considerable effort to clean up to the point of drinkability. The cabin itself only had the one door and windows on the front and sides. But the back wall was dominated by the old stove and stovepipe, otherwise bare, with no other exit. *I sure wouldn't want to get trapped in there,* Oswald thought.

Chapter 21

Shea and Waldschmidt rode into the small clearing by the cabin with guns drawn. They found Oswald leaning against the side of the cabin, apparently alone. He made no move to draw his gun.

"Harlan Shea," Oswald said.

"You're as good as dead, Oswald," Waldschmidt said. "How dare you strike my wife!"

"Hold your fire a moment, boys," Oswald said. "See, Louisa's in the cabin here. And if O'Connor hears any shooting, he's gonna kill her."

"You're bluffing. He'd never..." Shea began.

"Well, there's an easy way to find out," Oswald said, with an unpleasant laugh. "Look, Shea, either the little lady comes away nicely with us or she isn't going anywhere. Now, you're a nice fella, you wouldn't want to ruin things for this new little family in there. Say, maybe Mrs. O'Connor will even name you as her baby's godfather! That'd be awful special, wouldn't it?"

"Oswald, I'm not letting you take her," Shea said.

"And I'm not letting you off so easy, after what you did to Mary," Waldschmidt said.

"Then we have us a little dilemma here, don't we?" said Oswald, as Shea and Waldschmidt climbed down from their mounts. "Let the girl choose, then. Say, O'Connor, bring Louisa out here for a minute."

The door opened, and Louisa, still trussed up, shuffled out. O'Connor's gun was firmly planted against her head.

"Drop your weapons, boys, or I'll kill her," O'Connor said, his voice shaking.

"You're bluffing," Shea said, but the sight of Louisa's blackened eye, swollen face, and gagged mouth gave him

Trouble at Timber Ridge

pause. Shea and Waldschmidt hesitantly placed their guns at their feet.

"There now, that's better," Oswald said. As he prepared to remove her gag, he said, "Okay, Louisa, time to choose. Will you come away nicely with us?"

"Never!" she said fiercely. "Go ahead and kill me. I will never marry Alvis."

"Okay, then let me put this another way," Oswald said. He whipped out his gun and pointed it at Shea. "If you come away with us, Shea lives. Otherwise, I'll kill him right here in front of you."

Louisa's eyes were wide as she looked at Shea.

Suddenly there was a loud shriek, and a huge falcon swept down from the branches at Oswald's extended gun hand. Oswald tried to shoot Horace, but the shot went wild. Oswald dodged the bird, but lost his footing and fell on to the ground.

Shea and Oswald dove for their guns.

O'Connor swung his gun around, pointing from Shea to Waldschmidt and back, uncertain who he should fire at first.

Louisa, seizing the opportunity, threw her weight against him, knocking him off balance.

"Damn," Oswald snapped, and turned his gun toward Louisa.

With a feeling of dread for Louisa's safety, Shea bolted forward and tackled her, knocking her into the cover of the cabin.

Oswald's shot splintered the doorframe an inch from Shea's back.

Unnerved by the shooting, O'Connor darted for the trees, sending a few poorly aimed bullets whizzing in Waldschmidt's direction. Oswald sprang to his feet and turned his gun on Waldschmidt.

Waldschmidt fired at Oswald, and winged him in the arm. The wound wasn't severe, but bought Dan just enough time to dive into the cabin.

Thinking fast, Oswald grabbed a rifle from one of the horses and followed O'Connor to cover behind some trees, taking a position with good sight and range to cover the door of the cabin.

Inside the cabin, Shea swung the door closed and waited a moment as his eyes adjusted to the dimness. The sight of Louisa's pitiful condition awakened something dark in Shea; the fires of hell raged behind his eyes.

As he released her gag, the crack of a rifle echoed through the pines, followed by splintering wood.

Shea looked around, noted the lack of a back door, and the poorly slatted windows. He knelt at Louisa's side, and gently touched her dirty face with a huge paw.

"This feels awful familiar, Shea," Waldschmidt said. "Except it's her former lover rather than her Pa out there this time."

"If I gave myself up..." Louisa began.

"No," Shea interrupted.

"Hear me out, Harlan. If I gave myself up, do you think they'd stick to their bargain and let the two of you walk away?"

"No," Waldschmidt said flatly.

"But if they just want to take me home? There doesn't have to be any more shooting, does there? I mean, Alvis is just a boy who lost something and wants it back. Oswald wants to run the gang under the nose of the law. He just needs me to make the ranch look legitimate."

"Not just you he wants – he's after your Pa's loot," Dan suggested.

"What makes you so certain?" Louisa asked.

"Let's just call it a hunch."

"Pa never let on much to me about his outlaw days," Louisa said. "I know he had gold stashed here and there, but I learned at a young age not to ask questions. He wanted me to believe he was an honest rancher."

"Except for the score he had to settle with Haxton," Dan said.

"Except for that," Louisa agreed, ashamed.

An awkward silence ensued. Louisa's mind was clouded and confused. Her life, as she had known it since childhood, ended in the last twenty-four hours. Her father was gone, slain in the act of attempting to murder her lover. The latter, on the other hand, had become her kidnapper and tried to rob her of her inheritance. She knew Shea first as the robber of her mother's grave, and more recently as her father's killer. Now, he risked his life to come to her aid. She stared at him through the dim light.

"What do we do?" Louisa asked.

"We wait," Shea said, through gritted teeth.

"Louisa!" O'Connor called from the pines.

"Should I answer him?" she asked Waldschmidt.

"May as well," Waldschmidt said.

"What do you want?" she called.

"You've nowhere to run or hide," O'Connor called back. "You can't stay in there forever, and we've got guns on the door. Be a good girl and come out. I'll make sure Oswald lets Shea and Waldschmidt live. If not, well, you know what will happen."

"What choice do I have?" she asked, looking at Shea.

"Louisa, they can sit out there with their guns for quite some time, and not do a darned thing but wait," Waldschmidt said. "And we'll hunker down right here with you."

"I can't do that to you, to Mary," she said, her voice quivering. "The only chance you two get out of this alive is if I give myself up and go with them."

"I'll die before I let you go again," Shea said. "And don't fool yourself into thinking they'd let us off if you gave yourself up. They plan to kill us, one way or the other. Sacrificing yourself would accomplish nothing."

She looked at him with watery eyes. A long moment passed.

"I have some jerked beef in my pocket," Shea said. "That will last us a little while. Don't know what rations they have out there. Water is going to be a problem, though. Easier for them to get to than for us, I suppose, but it means one of them leaving for a spell.

"O'Connor out there, he's no experienced gunman. That means either they don't have us covered on all sides, or half the coverage is by a poor shot. Their voices are both coming from that way," he indicated with a finger, "generally speaking. We might be able to dig a way under this other wall and sneak out quietly, if they keep covering the door and window.

"Also, night's coming. Awful hard for them to aim in the dark. We could slip out right when night falls. Of course, Oswald knows that too. Likely, he'll try to force our hand before then. Maybe even torch the cabin. Point is, not to worry, this can't last too long."

"Shea's right," Waldschmidt said. "There's not much we can do but that would put us in greater jeopardy. Our best bet is to bank on their impatience, and wait for them to make a mistake. In the meantime, we might take shifts digging under this here wall."

Louisa slumped down in the corner, holding her head. "What a mess I've made of everything," she said."

"Don't fret, girl." Waldschmidt grinned tightly. "Trouble's like a shadow to Shea and me, isn't it, old boy? Follows us around like a stray puppy."

Shea grunted; he had no doubt about the truth of it.

The long afternoon was punctuated every hour or so by a shot at the door. Oswald's Winchester blew chunks out of the rotting wood, and the bullets embedded themselves in the far wall. One or two came mighty close to the captives, who kept low.

Shea and Waldschmidt took turns straining their eyes through the gaps in the mud plaster between the logs. Each rifle crack caused Louisa to jump, and her heart raced for several minutes afterward.

As dusk faded, an inky blackness encompassed the three in the little cabin. The damp evening chill pierced the gaps in the walls.

"I must have lived in town for too long," Louisa said. The confidence and strength of her voice gladdened Dan and thrilled Shea. "I've forgotten what real dark and quiet are like."

"Spent my childhood in a cabin in the woods just like this," Shea said. "Feels like home."

"Shea here grew up a trapper's son," Waldschmidt said. But remembering young Shea hunting down the men who killed his father sent a chill up his spine, he said no more.

Louisa's eyes stared into the pitch blackness, straining to see Shea, and comforted by the knowledge that she could do so unseen.

Chapter 22

Under the pines, Oswald shivered. Dark was coming, and that meant the possibility of escape for the three in the cabin. A coming frost was in the air and his nose and fingers became bitterly chilled. Occasionally, the whispers of the three inside carried on the wind which caused the pines to whistle. The whispers didn't suggest his quarry was any closer to giving up. Oswald knew he would have to bring this to a head soon.

-*- -*- -*-

Waldschmidt and Shea took turns digging and keeping vigil. The cold-hardened dirt of the cabin floor began to feel like rocks beneath their fingertips as they scooped away at the dirt beneath the cabin wall.

On one of Shea's watches, he silently pried open the slats across the windows. Still and patient as a stalking cat, he watched for the flash of a rifle in the darkness, and when it came, he let loose a volley into the dark pines.

Waldschmidt was on his feet in moments, gun drawn and aimed at the window where Shea had fired. Louisa stifled a scream and cowered into the corner by the stove. "Did you hit 'em?" Waldschmidt asked.

"No way to know," Shea said. "Didn't hear nothing that sounded like a wounded man, but dawn will tell for sure." The three strained their ears in the darkness, listening. Some minutes later, they heard a moan that sounded more like a man than a coyote.

"Nice shooting, Shea," Waldschmidt said.

"That's a man all right." Shea cautioned. "But that sound ain't coming from the direction I was shooting."

-*- -*- -*-

Trouble at Timber Ridge

The cold bothered Oswald the most. He rubbed his fingers to keep them from growing numb. He contemplated lighting a fire. "O'Connor," he said. "Run and grab those blankets off the horses."

O'Connor hid behind a thick pine trunk. "I'm not exposing myself to gunfire. Reckon I'm as good as your boss now, anyway. You go get the blankets, I'll cover the cabin."

"You're no use. What the hell am I keeping you alive for?"

"Right now, to help you keep those three pinned down in there," he said bitterly.

Oswald looked over his shoulder into the dark, remembering how thin this region of pine trees was, and how little cover they provided. The waiting was intolerable. Frustrated, Oswald aimed his rifle at the cabin door and pulled the trigger.

Instantly, from the side of the cabin came fireworks, and bullets whizzed by his ears.

O'Connor and Oswald fell on the pine needles, covering their heads. Shea's shots splintered wood close to Oswald's head and the air stank of burnt sap. "Damn it, Oswald, they can see the muzzle flash! Stop shooting, you'll get us killed for sure."

"Shut up, O'Connor," Oswald said, knowing the former telegrapher was right. "We best shift our position, since now they know where we are. We'll have to take cover closer to the front door. By the horses, maybe."

As they crept through the dimly lit trees, they heard a moan, obviously from a human. "What the devil's that?" O'Connor whispered.

"Don't know," Oswald said.

"You think you hit one of them?"

"That sound ain't coming from inside the cabin." The moaning was periodic, coming and going with the breeze.

Oswald was quiet for a moment, then swore violently. "Those flashes, those might have been from the side of the cabin. Damn it, they may be out already."

"What the hell do we do now?"

"You follow that sound, O'Connor. See if the injured man is with the girl. I'll check the cabin and make sure it's empty."

O'Connor crept between the trees, surprised how quickly he could cover ground in the darkness. Periodically, he would pause and wait to hear the wounded man again. Soon he was some distance from the cabin, and the sound was close. In the fast-failing light of the setting sun, he could see the shadow of a man stumbling between the trees. He crept up cautiously behind the injured man, holding a pistol shakily in front of him.

_*_ _*_ _*_

Oswald made his way through the shadowy twilight to the door of the cabin. He lay his rifle on the ground and drew both of his revolvers. He needed to see inside. At least one of them had gotten out, he was sure. He strained to peek through the cracks between the logs, but it was pitch black inside.

It would be suicide to open the door, Oswald thought. *I'll fire the cabin.*

Withdrawing a few paces, Oswald concealed himself behind a pine. Mainly by touch, he amassed some dried branches as kindling and struck a match. The kindling took quickly. The pine oil in the twigs lit fast and burned bright. In the glow of the small fire, he could see some fatter branches a few steps away. He realized his danger, and hurried to light them, while sheltering as much of himself as he could behind a thin pine.

But, as he held the sticks over the fire, a revolver fired from between the cabin logs. The shot whizzed by and kicked up dirt a few feet away. It was quickly followed by another, which thudded heavily into the tree beside him. With the third, the heavy thud of a bullet struck him in the side. Gingerly, he touched the wound. His shirt already felt damp and warm.

There was no pain, not yet; the shock numbed it. A torrent of images flashed though Oswald's mind. He thought of White Pines, with its vast acreage and clumps of cottonwoods. He thought of the ranch house with its

Trouble at Timber Ridge

secret stores of wealth. And he thought of Louisa, hanging on the fence rails, her hair blowing in the wind. *Damn it, Louisa,* he thought, *if I can't have you, no one will!*

He could feel weakness spreading in his limbs. He shuffled up to the door of the cabin. With a furious kick, he knocked the thin door in. Louisa screamed from where she crouched in a corner.

Despite stumbling a bit as he crashed through the door, Oswald fired wildly. Shea and Waldschmidt, already on their feet, immediately returned fire. Bullets flew around the cabin, splintering wood. Waldschmidt grunted. In a moment, it was over. A tense silence fell over the cabin.

"Dan?" Louisa said. "Harlan?"

"You all right, Louisa?" Shea asked.

"Oh, thank God, Harlan. Are you all right?"

"I'm hit," he said. His voice was calm coming out of the darkness. "But Dan took it worse than me."

"Dan?" She felt around on the floor for Waldschmidt, found his head, and cradled it in her lap. "Dan, say something! Please!"

"We got him, Louisa," Waldschmidt choked, as a spasm of bloody coughing racked his broken form. "I saw him fall. We got him."

Chapter 23

In the dimly lit woods, O'Connor crept up behind his quarry, rifle held awkwardly, unfamiliar in his soft hands. He intended not to alert the man to his presence until he was just behind him, knowing full well his aim was poor and the man may be armed.

Suddenly, from a distance behind him, he heard volleys of gunfire at the cabin. A million thoughts flashed through O'Connor's mind. If Oswald was dead, where did that leave him?

The shadowy man spun. O'Connor found himself face to face with a terrible visage, stained with blood and filth. Empty, eyeless sockets stared at him in the dim light. The tattered lips parted and a terrible moan escaped the gaping maw. O'Connor gasped.

"That you, Oswald?" Henry asked. Vacant sockets bored into O'Connor's eyes. "I can't see. That devil Shea, his bird..."

_-*- -*- -*-_

As night set in, wolves howled in the distance, and the horses snorted and stomped in agitation. Louisa went out to get water from the spring. She took a canteen and the bedrolls off the horses. With substantial effort, she unsaddled them, and took the saddle blankets as well. Then, she untied the horses so they could wander the small clearing and eat what grass was available to them. Spooked by the wolves, they took off. She cursed her luck. Outside, she tore fragments from her dress and tried to use the cloth to fill a canteen with clean water. But the cloth was soon choked with mud.

Waldschmidt had taken two bullets through the gut, and she doubted very much if he would live long enough to see Mary again. This broke her heart – she wished

Trouble at Timber Ridge

terribly she could ride into town and bring her back. Several times she considered getting on a horse. But the night was growing dark and would be moonless, and the trail overgrown. Even if she could find her way back to town, the return trip would be impossible.

She decided to wait until first light, and then ride back to the Waldschmidts' ranch to get Mary. It might soothe the woman's soul to be with her husband when he crossed into the Hereafter.

She took some wood and lit a fire in the stove, providing some light and warmth in the small, cold room. She looked over at Shea, unconscious in the corner. He had taken a bullet through the shoulder. She wondered how he would fare if she rode off to get help.

Outside, a cold October drizzle had begun, and she kicked herself for not gathering more dry wood earlier. She drenched herself wetting strips of cloth with freezing rain to clean Shea's wound. At least the rain provided clean drinking water. Having no funnel, she was forced to catch it directly in the neck of the canteen. She had never felt so alone or so miserable than when standing amidst the pines holding the slender-neck canteen to the heavens, thankful the freezing rain was there to mask her tears.

Returning to the cabin, she felt a spark of hope as she found Shea sitting up by the stove. "Harlan, I'm so happy you're awake," she said. "But I don't want to see you moving around just yet."

"I won't," he uttered, just audibly.

She noticed he was holding the barrel of his revolver into the fire, the butt wrapped in cloth. The tip glowed red hot.

"Can't have this shoulder get infected," he said. He pulled the gun from the fire and lay back down.

Louisa turned away as he slapped the hot barrel on the wound. She did not hear him utter a sound, just the sizzle of flesh, and then the thud of the heavy gun onto the packed dirt floor. She went out into the cold rain and was sick.

Recovering her wits, she thought to carry more wood to shelter, while the smell of freshly seared flesh dissipated. She gathered what she could feel out in the dark. It was damp, and a thin layer of ice was beginning to form. Returning, she stopped just paces from the cabin door, hearing the men talking quietly inside.

"Tell her, Shea." Waldschmidt coughed, a bloody sound. "Tell her the truth!"

"Save your strength, man," Shea said.

"Yes, Dan, please don't overexert yourself," Louisa urged, hurrying in and kneeling beside him.

"Shea didn't rob your Pa, Louisa," Waldschmidt managed with considerable effort.

"It doesn't matter now, Dan," Shea insisted.

Waldschmidt moaned.

He was fading fast, and Louisa knew it. She tore another fragment from her skirt and used it to dry the sweat and filth from the dying man's face. A tear rolled down her cheek, and along the smooth line of her jaw. "Easy, Dan," she said, choking back a sob. "We can talk later. Mary's waiting for you back home. I'll get her here first thing in the morning. We'll get you home."

"No," Waldschmidt rasped, "you won't. I'm dying ... don't take me for a fool."

She gripped his hand in both of hers and squeezed firmly. "You were so kind to me. I'll always remember."

"Mary'll need caring for. Might be some time before the ranch sells."

"I'll take her with me to White Pines. Heaven knows, I'll need her help when the baby comes."

"Louisa," Waldschmidt whispered, then a spasm of coughing racked his broken form. "Harlan didn't rob your Pa. I did. Oswald and I, we planned it together. Harlan, he took the blame for me. We orphans, we ... we stick together ... Louisa, I'm sorry ..."

Moments later, after a painful spasm of coughing, he died.

_*_ _*_ _*_

Trouble at Timber Ridge

As the night continued, the ground froze. Wolves howled mournfully in the dark, closing in fast on the smell of death.

She sought comfort by Shea's side. She watched the steady breathing of his huge chest, and felt the muscles of his arm against her soft cheek. She drew herself to her knees and uncovered his wounded shoulder. The flesh was red and angry.

"How does it look?" he asked.

"Better," she lied. "How does it feel?"

"Like I'm lucky to be alive," he said.

She tore another shred off her shrinking skirt and used it to replace his blood-soaked bandage. Then, without thinking, she suddenly leaned forward and kissed his forehead. It was warm and salty with sweat. She drew back, but his coarse, uninjured hand caught her fair cheek and drew her lips to his. He caressed her silky, disheveled hair.

Her senses awoke with a rush of heat she had never experienced. She wanted desperately to surrender herself to him, this mysterious gunfighter, this killer, and it sickened and thrilled her. After several long minutes, she pulled back a few inches and turned her eyes away. She winced as she looked at the dead man's face, half-uncovered under the blanket.

"Louisa," Shea began.

"Harlan, you should rest." On hands and knees, she crossed the floor and pulled the blanket up so it covered Waldschmidt's head. Then, she curled up in front of the stove with her back to Shea, and cried quietly.

The night passed slowly. She dozed again briefly, but was awakened by the sound of growling outside. Cautiously, she took one of Shea's heavy guns in both her hands and crept to the doorway. In the dim light that leaked out of the broken door of the cabin, she saw snarling gray shapes and glistening eyes moving about Oswald's dead form.

"Wolves?" Shea asked, sitting up.

"How horrible," she said.

"It's a fate better than he deserved," Shea replied. "I imagine the horses spooked and ran off. We'll make for Timber Ridge on foot at first light."

"Are you fit enough?"

"Don't matter none. I'll have to do it. I can rest up back in town."

They dozed again to the sound of feeding wolves, rending joints and tearing flesh. She barricaded the cabin doorway as best she could with the broken door, the now useless saddles, and some branches she had dragged in for firewood. She bound them together with saddle straps. It wasn't much of a barrier, but she hoped it would keep the wolves away from Dan's body for a while.

When they awoke, the wolves were gone and the rising sun lit a crisp morning. They crawled out through the window, as the door was barricaded, closing the shutters behind them. At the sight of Oswald's mangled form, Louisa was sick again.

Shea took off his coat and wrapped it around Louisa before he examined the barricade in the doorway, and then dragged a few more branches to add to it.

"Will that hold?" Louisa asked.

"Hush!" Shea cocked his head, listening. "Quickly," he whispered, and grabbing her wrist, he led her into the woods behind the cabin.

Chapter 24

Mary rubbed her tired eyes as she stared hopelessly down the path to town from the porch of the modest cabin that had been a warm and loving home for her and her husband. In her heart, she knew Dan was never coming home. She also knew Harlan Shea had much to do with it. As soon as her husband had said Shea's name, she knew trouble was on its way. Men like Shea attracted evil like a rotting carcass drew flies. It was not that she assumed Shea was inherently a malevolent influence. Rather, the fates of men like him were inextricably tied to those of evil men. Shea was cursed, this Mary was sure of.

Mary returned inside, tears streaming down her cheeks. What would she do if her Dan never came through the front door again? She said a quick prayer, grabbed her shawl, and headed out, down the path to town. The cabin sounded so quiet and empty that she couldn't stand to be alone.

-*- -*- -*-

Alvis O'Connor was cold, wet, and miserable as he led blind Henry through the pines to where he thought Timber Ridge was. Why he took the disabled man along with him, he could not say. But, O'Connor was a man undergoing a powerful change. He was finished being walked over and ordered around. With his wits, he knew he was capable of great things. Moreover, he had a gnawing hunger for retribution against the many folks who had wronged him of late.

Henry had been, until recently, a quite intimidating man, O'Connor reflected. He was a large man with a low-slung jaw and a protruding eyebrow ridge that suggested low intelligence and limited self-control. These traits, which only days before would have caused O'Connor to cower in his presence, now filled him with a sense of pride and a newfound confidence, albeit somewhat muted by his lost, soaked and shivering condition. O'Connor was winning the trust of a vicious killer; a strong man and experienced outlaw relied on him for guidance. O'Connor had a henchman, albeit a maimed one, and he liked the feeling of power it gave him.

Of course, O'Connor's imagination flattered him. The two looked quite ridiculous, wandering about in circles under the pines, the gangly city boy in stained vest and tie, absurdly overconfident in his sense of direction holding the hand of the blind, bandaged gargantuan in a ragged coat, who kept bumping his head on low-hanging branches.

During the night, they had slept, cold and hungry, on wet pine needles as wolves howled in the distance. When dawn broke, they resumed their lost wandering. It wasn't long before, by luck, O'Connor stumbled on the trail between town and the cabin, and he smiled at his good fortune. The sun was beginning to warm them as O'Connor led his charge up the trail.

When they came to the clearing in which the cabin sat, O'Connor suppressed his surprise but swore to himself. He had thought they were headed toward town, and he cursed himself for heading up the trail the wrong way. He parked blind Henry at the wood line and cautiously approached the cabin on tiptoes, clutching the rifle like a security blanket. There was a body lying by the door of the cabin, so badly gnawed and torn O'Connor barely recognized it as Oswald. Alvis quickly turned away, bracing himself with his hands on his knees, until the nausea passed. Their horses were gone.

Over the barricade in the cabin door, O'Connor could see that the room was empty, except for a body lying by the wall. O'Connor opened the window slats and crawled through. He pulled back the saddle blanket and muttered, "Damn," when he recognized Dan Waldschmidt. Waldschmidt had a reputation in town as a good man, and he and his brother Cody were well-liked.

Trouble at Timber Ridge

What a shame he had died like this. The stove was still warm, although the fire had all but burned out, and he stood for a moment warming his icy fingers before returning to the clearing.

"Where the hell are we?" Henry called, growing impatient and annoyed.

"Oswald's dead," O'Connor said, crawling back out through the window.

"Well, where does that leave us?" Henry asked.

A voice called from the woods, "You there!" Both men spun on their heels. "You been here long?"

"Who's there?" O'Connor responded.

"Name's Benson. Deputy Sheriff of Lonsdale. We're looking for somebody. Perhaps you know him." Several men stepped out from behind the trees.

"Who's that you're looking for?" O'Connor asked.

"Harlan Shea."

"What for?"

"He gunned down our sheriff and several of our most respected citizens."

"You don't say," O'Connor replied, thinking fast. "It just so happens we're looking for him as well."

"That body at your feet have something to do with him?"

"That there was our boss."

"Looks like wolves got him pretty good."

"Shea shot him and left him for wolf bait."

Benson shifted his rifle to his left side and extended his right hand. "What's your handle?"

"Alvis O'Connor."

"And who's the blind feller there?" Benson asked.

"Why, that's Henry. And Harlan Shea owes him his eyes." He paused. "Mind if I ride with you and help see this thing done right?"

"What about your friend?" He pointed to Henry.

O'Connor felt guilty leaving blind Henry alone in the woods, but the chance to ride with Benson's posse and be in on the kill when they took down Shea was too much of a temptation. "I'll get someone from town to see to him."

Benson considered.

"I know the town and its folk," Alvis added. "I might be of some assistance to you."

Benson shrugged. "Fine." He turned and walked off toward the horses. "If you can find yourself a horse. But first, we search these woods. See, there's a hint of smoke coming out of that stovepipe yet. They couldn't have gone far."

Chapter 25

A few yards from the cabin, crouching in a clump of rocks and scrub brush, Shea whispered in Louisa's ear, "Look, they're tying up their horses. They're gonna fan out and search the woods on foot. We'll keep down here and make for the horses when they've spread out a mite."

"Oh, Harlan, that was close. I didn't even hear them coming. How's your shoulder?" She began troubling his shirt near the bullet wound, but he gently removed her hands.

"I'll be all right. I can get about okay, and I can shoot with my good arm, should I need to."

"We'll never get out of here, will we, Harlan? They'll find us for sure."

Shea shushed her gently. "Well, it's gonna be tricky, that's true." Harlan drew a massive revolver from a holster on his unwounded side. Moisture from the soggy leaves seeped into their clothes, making them shiver. Shea sat squarely on his haunches, his head cocked to one side, listening.

When he felt fairly certain the searchers had scattered and would no longer hear their footfalls in the leaves, he took Louisa's hand and they bolted for the horses. Shea fairly threw her on one of the posse mounts, slapped its rump, and sent her rocketing down the trail.

-*- -*- -*-

The noise of the horse crashing along the overgrown trail attracted the posse's attention, and the men began shouting as they raced for their horses. A bullet hissed over Shea's head as he leapt onto a second mount. Half-turned in his saddle, Shea let loose a single shot that reduced the number of pursuers by one soul.

Moments later, the posse men were riding out, fast. O'Connor felt a sinking feeling in his stomach as he glanced back at Henry, who shouted, "Alvis! Alvis! Where are you?"

"I'll send someone back for you," O'Connor yelled.

-*- -*- -*-

When Shea and Louisa broke free of the woods and out into the open, Shea caught up. His horse was running shoulder-to-shoulder with Louisa's. "They're after me, Louisa, for some men I killed back in Lonsdale. Head to O'Malley's or Mary's or anywhere and hide. I'll lose them in the mountains."

"I'm not leaving your side, Harlan Shea. I'm going to White Pines, and you're coming with me. I don't care if danger follows, you won't leave me again."

"O'Connor is with them. He might lead the Lonsdale men down to Texas, but one way or the other, I don't think you'll be getting much of a welcome at White Pines. We'll figure a way to take the ranch back, but first, I have to shake these boys." Glancing over his shoulder, he saw the posse emerging from the woods perhaps a hundred yards behind them. "It's too late, they've seen us together, and now they're likely to arrest you if they catch you. We'll make for higher ground together."

The two riders raced around the back of the main street stores. O'Malley, hearing the thundering hooves, stepped out of the back kitchen and onto the stoop behind the saloon as they passed. Shea and Louisa slowed their horses briefly as they passed O'Malley.

"Dan's dead," Shea yelled. "Up the trail."

"I'll take care of it," O'Malley yelled back.

"Look after Mary," Louisa hollered.

"It'll be done," the barkeep promised.

Moments after Harlan and Louisa cleared the edge of town, the remaining horsemen roared after them. O'Connor rode with them on the dead Lonsdale man's horse.

They passed fields of cattle that spooked and stampeded. Shea knew it was foolish to keep the horses running at this pace on such rocky, uneven trails, but

Trouble at Timber Ridge

there was nothing else to do. He had to keep Louisa safe. She led the way, and he followed closely.

Behind them, Benson's posse tore through the scraggly pines and past boulders strewn maddeningly about by long receded glaciers. Around one bend, Benson ducked as a shrieking monstrosity swooped so low over his head that he lost his hat. The man behind him bore the impact of sharp talons, fell from his horse, to be trampled by the horse behind him.

As the trees thinned, Shea realized their pace was slowing and the posse was closing in on firing range. As they galloped through diminishing cover, shots were fired from behind. Shea urged the horses on, despite the uneven ground. He and Louisa scampered up treacherous rockslides and skidded down loose soil and stone. "I don't know how long we can keep this up, Louisa," Shea yelled. "There's a pass up ahead, and beyond that a wooded hollow. I have a place there, if we can make it."

A few yards from the mouth of the pass, Shea's horse let out a terrible scream as her leg snapped and she crashed to the ground. Louisa heard the injured horse's scream, and jerked her horse to a halt. "Harlan!"

"I'm all right," Shea growled. "But she's done for. Go on, Louisa! Go, damn it, they're gaining. I'll buy you some time." He raised a revolver toward the on-coming posse.

"I won't leave you, Harlan."

"Louisa, there's no time. Go!"

"Harlan Shea, you get on this horse!"

She sat straight and proud in the saddle, a strong, beautiful woman. Framed by the towering walls of the pass beyond, she looked more gorgeous than he had ever seen her. And Shea knew then that he loved her. He hesitated just a minute, and turned to his horse. Her left foreleg was broken, and he knew she had run her last. "I'm sorry, old girl," he said, and he shot her behind the eye.

Then he ran.

Shea swung into the saddle behind Louisa and they charged into the pass. The posse was gaining fast, followed by O'Connor, who had gained a little on the group when Horace had impaired their progress. Coming around the bend, rifles raised, they fired volley after volley at the fleeing couple, now only a few yards distant. Shea reined the horse, straining under the weight of two riders at a trot, and craned his neck to check on the posse's progress.

The posse followed until Benson held out his arms to stop their fire. He had quickly realized the peril: Gunfire could send the piles of snow hundreds of feet above them crashing down on their heads.

"Home's just there, in the woods beyond the pass," Shea spoke into her ear.

Home, she thought, cherishing the word. "But won't we be trapped there?"

Shea didn't answer.

The posse entered the pass, but were moving tentatively, their many eyes fixed on the towering cliffs and precarious snow fields and boulders above. Shea looked over his shoulder again and smiled grimly. He and Louisa would not be overtaken before the woods.

"Get ready," he whispered in Louisa's ear.

"For what?" she asked.

"Unleashed hell."

They were some distance yet from the wood when the giant gunfighter raised his revolvers and, wincing slightly from the pain, lifted both to the sky. The guns spoke, and the heavens responded.

A low rumble, like distant thunder, reverberated through the narrow pass, quickly rising to a roar. Harshly, Shea kicked the steed into a furious pace. The horse, sensing the imminent danger, needed little encouragement. They raced on between the collapsing walls of snow. Boulders rained down into the pass. Some men struggled to turn their horses and break for the mouth while others raced madly after Shea and Louisa.

O'Connor slammed his horse to a halt and watched as the pass was obliterated, becoming an insurmountable wall of ice and rubble as horses and riders were lost in a blizzard of white death. He watched as his rash plan of ill-conceived vengeance was swallowed by the pass. His

Trouble at Timber Ridge

horse reared, throwing him in a muddled heap. Waves of snow washed over him and he fought desperately to keep his head above the rising torrent.

As Shea and Louisa raced though the pass, he could feel every muscle of the horse's body straining beneath them. Froth from its mouth sprayed back in their faces, and its coat glistened with sweat, in spite of the cold. Louisa lowered her head and closed her eyes, holding the saddle horn tightly as the horse jerked suddenly to one side, narrowly missing a massive boulder. She thought she was screaming, but could not hear her own voice above the cacophony. Yard by yard, they raced through the disintegrating pass toward the wood line where the refuge of his cabin lay. Giant tongues of snow lapped at the floor of the pass on all sides. The air filled with white, freezing clouds and stinging shards of rock.

Behind them, pillars of snow rained down on the posse. Benson was thrown when his horse fell over a tumbling boulder. He scrambled to his feet, only to be smothered in a cold, terminal embrace. One by one, the posse drowned in the fury of falling mountains.

Suddenly, Shea and Louisa burst from the crumbling pass and the shadows of the wood engulfed them. Shea brought the blowing mount to a halt as the thunder died out behind them. The walls of snow and stone had closed the pass, entombing their pursuers. The new silence was broken by the high-pitched call of a giant falcon as Horace glided over them.

They were sealed in, at least until the spring thaw. But there was plenty of game and dry wood, and the cabin was stocked with supplies from his most recent stay. They would be fine through the winter, and when spring came, he could fetch up the doctor to deliver the baby. The long months of winter would give him plenty of time to plan taking White Pines back from the gang who undoubtedly would claim it. And down in Texas, no one would even have heard of Lonsdale.

Louisa held his arms against her and nuzzled her head beneath his stubbly chin. Easing around slightly in the saddle, she turned her face up to his and their lips met.

_*_ _*_ _*_

The feud was over, Louisa reflected as they rode through the haunting stillness of the woods. The shackles of the last generation's disputes had fallen from their ankles, and for the first time in her life, Louisa felt in command of her own destiny. The future was theirs to decide, theirs for the taking. She was no longer her father's pawn in his schemes of vengeance and sin. She was free from her cowardly would-be fiancé, whose soul had been blackening with each passing hour. She was safe in the wild desolation of the mountains behind the frozen bulwark, held firmly in the arms of her half-savage lover. The warmth of his immense body comforted her as they rode to the cabin.

The strength of his arms thrilled her as he lifted her lightly from their mount and carried her as easily as he might a small child across the threshold of his simple, rustic cabin home.

Their home – at least for now.

The End

About the Author

Kevin Crisp teaches college biology and has authored some fifteen science research papers and textbook chapters. He has also published short stories in the western and horror genres in eZines such as Frontier Tales and the Lovecraft eZine.

Kevin received his BA in psychology from Haverford College and a PhD in neuroscience from the University of Minnesota. He also studied anatomy at University College of London in England and physiology at the University of Miami in Florida.

Born and raised outside of Washington, D.C., Kevin has been living in a small town in Minnesota for eight years.

Visit Kevin on *Google* at
http://plus.google.com/107872475806183452447/

Made in the USA
San Bernardino, CA
07 April 2014